ROSS ALEXANDER

For A, A & E

AUTHOR'S NOTE

This is a work of fiction. Names and characters are the product of the author's imagination and any resemblance to actual persons, living or dead, is entirely coincidental.

2011 Diary of Stephen James Hamilton

Saturday January 1st

Happy New Year or so I feel obligated to begin.

I start this year in a state of confound confusion. You see, I think that I'm an ordinary person, nothing extraordinary has ever happened, or tends to happen in my life. I see myself as an ordinary guy in his mid-thirties. I have an ordinary job; live in an ordinary flat in an ordinary part of the city. I have ordinary friends, have had ordinary relationships with females (albeit, not at present) and my days currently run from one ordinary moment to another. So why is it that this year I'm to be murdered?

Let me explain further.

I received a hand delivered note through my letter box at some point last night. To document the message verbatim, it states –

'Enjoy as much of this year as you can, for it is to be your last'

The message has been typed (Times New Roman) on an A4 sheet of plain white paper. That's it.

At first it came as a bit of a shock, however, I blame my initial reaction solely on my Hogmanay hangover. After reflection in the cold light of day (and a number of Extra Power Paracetamol) I know that this is obviously a hoax, some kind of sick joke from one of the guys from last night. I have, therefore, decided on my plan of action – inaction.

The group that I socialise with do enjoy the occasional prank or practical joke and I often join in with them. Time will soon reveal the guilty prankster, or indeed if this whole affair relates to something far more sinister.

Sunday January 2nd

In all the excitement of writing my first entry into this diary, I forgot to note my New Years Resolutions for the coming year. These resolutions were duly announced to the guys at the Hogmanay Party, so here goes –

1 – Do not take drugs.
2 – Eat less junk food.
3 – Drink less (alcohol).
4 – Drink more water (2 litres per day, so I have been informed).
5 – Exercise more.
6 – Write a diary entry each and every day.
7 – Try not to get murdered.

OK, so I added the last one today, however, it's still relevant I feel and it does bring my total up to a 'Magnificent Seven'. I think I should take this opportunity to document the reasons behind Resolution number six. Last Christmas my old university chum, Alex Simpson, gave me this diary. He has challenged me to complete this diary for the year ahead and has staked £100 of his hard earned cash that I will not be able to do it. Alex is an artist, poet and writer, although not necessarily in that order. He does; however, seem to have the ability to make ends meet. I have always had an appreciation of the arts myself; however, music has always been my thing. I reached grade five on the piano before I became influenced by other vices that distract you in senior high school. I can also play a few tunes on the violin and the guitar, although, I do not own a violin (or have touched one in about fifteen years) and my guitar only gets an airing in times of extreme boredom (the last time was about 3 months ago).

Anyway, Alex is always encouraging me to write (he has seen my attempts at drawing – a complete and sincere lost cause apparently). He has this ever mounting belief that there is a book in me somewhere ('a work of literary classicism' or so he says). I'm not too sure, however, in a bid to stop him badgering me, I have reluctantly agreed to start with this diary (plus I cannot afford to lose another drunken bet to him, so much more than just the money at stake you understand).

So, after day two, I am still on track for the cash, just finished the last of my two litres of water, abstained from consuming drugs, alcohol and junk food, and went for a two mile run (jog/walk call it what you want) before dinner.

Oh, and I'm still alive, so it's so far so good…………..

Monday January 3rd

I met with Alex for lunch today (Falafels washed down with orange juice) and told him to get his £100 ready as after two days of writing I'm on a roll. He stated that I was to 'be free with my writing' whatever that is suppose to mean. He also said that it should be personal to me and he had no intention of reading it. The knowledge that I was writing was good enough for him apparently. He himself has many fingers in many pies at present. He is currently working on a large commissioned painting for 'an exceedingly wealthy lawyer from the depths of Edinburgh's affluent society' (Morningside, then) which in his humble option is 'a fine example of pretentious nonsense'. I think the £5k commission fee is sufficient to bypass his artistic filtering system. He is also currently finishing his third novel 'bound to be snapped up by a publisher – piece of sheer genius' having resorted to self publishing his first two efforts. I must record, however, that in my opinion both were excellent. Based in an Edinburgh theatre, the first was a comical whodunit and the second a romantic tale (not usually my cup of tea, however, found I could not put it down). He is also working on a screenplay for a short film that has 'Cannes written all over it'. Alex has a rule of never discussing specifics regarding his work in progress unless, of course, it is a work of pretentious nonsense.

I must admit, that for a minute I did consider discussing the threatening note with him, however, I am maintaining my inaction strategy. I do think that this is the work of one of the guys, although do not think Alex is involved. Alex tends to go for the more intellectual pranks such as the time I received a call from the Political Editor of The Scotsman wanting comments on my move into politics. Alex's pranks also tend to be undertaken solely ('I will never work as part of a group of inadequate mentality') and only revealed at a later time. I shall await the big climax if he turns out to be involved after all.

After we parted, I went for a stroll along the canal bank to gather my thoughts. I only planned to walk for half an hour, however, I didn't return to the flat until three hours later. Topics for current thought are –

1 – Back to work tomorrow – Is this what I want to do for the rest of my life?
2 – Relationship – Currently single, is it time to change this?
3 – Health – Get this sorted before you turn 40.
4 – Writing – What type of book would I write if this diary thing takes off?

I surprised myself in three counts after dinner. Firstly, I made a healthy meal for myself without thinking, am I really changing this quickly? Secondly, I picked up my guitar and played for about an hour, and I was not even bored. Finally, I got ready for bed at 9 o'clock, just so I could write today's entry.

Maybe there is method in Alex's madness after all…

Tuesday January 4th

Back to work today, having enjoyed a long and peaceful sleep for a change. I work as a Senior Underwriter at one of the large insurance companies based in Edinburgh. Not my ideal job by any stretch of the imagination, however, it pays well and the office is close to my flat. I oversee a team of five Underwriters and report (when I must) to Margaret Watson (from hereon referred to as Darth Vader). Darth is from the old school of office management whereas she gets things done, but rubs most people up the wrong way in the process. She likes me, for some reason, so I am left to get on with it. I, in turn, let my staff do their own job (we are all grown ups after all) and only get involved if there is a problem. As such, the team seem quite happy and don't give me too much grief.

The day panned out pretty much uneventfully and I decided to leave the office just after five o'clock which doesn't happen that often. I decided to have another stroll along the canal bank as the weather is holding up at present, much to the surprise of the residents of Edinburgh. The usual Arctic gale that we 'enjoy' is currently hidden which made the hour long stroll more pleasant that normal. Conditions are best described as being 'fresh', which is another way of saying that it is absolutely freezing, but dry.

After dinner, I called Wills to firm up on our arrangements for tomorrow; however, he was out so I just left a message. We usually head for a game of snooker on a Wednesday night, trying not to drink too much on a school night. More times than not we fail miserably, so I need to keep myself away from the bar and take a wide berth past the kebab shop on the way home.

Wednesday January 5th

Darth decided to have a 'breakfast meeting' at 8 o'clock this morning, so I brought along a black pudding and haggis double roll just to annoy her (the smell was outrageous, but the taste…). I must admit I'm not really a morning person and don't usually function properly until 10 o'clock. I took the 'nod your head and agree with everything she says' approach today, which got me through to the meetings conclusion. To be honest, the subject matter covered at today's meeting was identical to the last three.

After falling off the healthy eating wagon, I decided to go all out and have a meatball sandwich at lunch and a burger meal for dinner before I meet Wills for a game of snooker. Somehow, I knew that alcohol would need absorbing.

Jack 'Wills' Matthews is another friend from university, however, is completely different from Alex. He has no appreciation for the arts, although, he is a self titled 'Piss Artist of the Highest Order'. Wills has never settled down with a proper job and moves from one temporary job to another ('plenty of time for all that settling down rubbish later'). He acts as if he is still a student, hence his nickname 'Wills' (after the famous 'University Outfitters').

We met outside the snooker club at 8 and I could tell he was fine mood. Wills is a handsome guy, tall at 6 foot 3, well built from his rugby days at school and is always well groomed. Wills wears sunglasses whatever the weather (as an overpriced Alice band when the sun is not out) and I think this is more to prevent self-blinding from his Hollywood white teeth.

We called time on the snooker at a quarter to eleven with the match finely poised at three frames each. We are not overly competitive, so we are both generally happy when it ends in a draw. I did manage to absorb a few beers, however, did abstain from the shots of Jack Daniels that Wills moved on to. I did not, however, manage the wide berth of the take away shop and have just finished the last of my large Doner Kebab. I hope that today's entry has not been too badly affected by my consumptions.

Man, am I going to pay for this in the morning.

Thursday January 6th

I managed to drag myself into work this morning having contemplated working from home. Darth is in London for a meeting and not due back until Monday so it turned out a wise move on my part. I spent much of the first hour on the toilet, that kebab was definitely not up to the usual standards of catering hygiene, but the alcohol prevented me noticing until it had been fully consumed. I held a team meeting late afternoon, more to check everyone was without complaint rather than for any specific business reason. The only problem raised was the water cooler is stuck at nineteen degrees Celsius, but no one had the initiative to call the facilities management team. Brownie points for me then for getting the issue resolved this evening before they come in tomorrow.

I phoned Wills before I left work to check up on his hangover status. 'No problem mate, up at six this morning, had a ten kilometre run and into work for nine'. I swear he is immune to hangovers. All is quiet on his relationship side, which is highly unusual. This either means he is between girlfriends (should they be called partners at our age?) or he is quite serious about his current one.

I stopped at my usual coffee shop on the way home to read over some paperwork. Surprisingly, I found myself ordering a skinny latte for a change which raised an eyebrow from my regular Barista. I often have a quick chat with her, she is quite attractive, dark hair, tall, slim with a great accent (Eastern European, not sure where though, possibly Polish). I spend an hour or so reading through the paperwork, however, my mind was wandering and I found myself contemplating asking for a date. My concern is her age, I am hopeless at telling peoples age; she could be 19 or 39 for all I know. She does seem mature so could be closer to my age, but for the time being I decided to leave this on the backburner. I did notice her glace towards me a few times, and she smiled at me at least once. Is there something there perhaps, or is she looking for another sale/tip?

Back to healthy eating today and I drank three litres of water. Is it bad for you to drink too much water? With the amount of hydrating I needed this morning, I suspect today did not matter so much.

Friday January 7th

I let the team away at four o'clock today and left myself just after five. I like to do this from time to time as it makes me come across as a considerate, thoughtful boss. I am happy for this illusion to be maintained at present. In truth, nothing much happens in the last hour of a Friday, so it gives me a chance to catch up and prepare for the following week. I received an e-mail from Darth just before I left; she appears extremely upset at something that happened in London. I just hope it has nothing to do with me, however when it does she always lets me know straight away. I think this has only happened twice in five years.

I decided to pop over to see Dad this evening; however, he was not at home. More than likely he would be down at the bowling club, so I let myself in and left him a note (I personally couldn't face the bowling club tonight – still not fully recovered from Wednesday night). After writing the note, I found myself sitting at the piano. I've not played since I was at university so needed to blow away some cobwebs. I must have played for two hours, mostly Mozart (by far my favourite composer) and a few tunes I made up myself as I went along. I wonder if it too late to complete my grades, however, I'm sure even if I wanted to I would never find the time.

I now realise that the last time I played I had just finished first year at Edinburgh University, which was also around the time Mum died. She succumbed to breast cancer, aged just fifty six – I was completely devastated. A lonely child, I had to grow up fast (although a fully grown adult, I was very much still looked after by my parents). I've always been very close to them and, since I moved out, spent most Sundays at the house I grew up in. I shall continue to do this until…

I finished the evening in front of the television watching a late night European film. I have absolutely no idea what happened as I drifted off a few times throughout and missed the ending completely. I decided to write this after a large late night coffee, which took me back again to my Barista.

I'm sure sweet dreams await me.

Saturday January 8th

I've now made my made my mind up in relation to my Barista (as I can no longer refer to her in these terms). I have set myself a challenge which will result in the asking for a date (or not). To reach this point, I am to discover the following facts about her –

1 – Her name (seems a good place to start.)

2 – Her age (at my age I think plus or minus 10 years is the maximum)
3 – Is she single?

Obviously, the last question is compulsory before I make a complete idiot of myself (although that may happen regardless).

I think this decision was partly due to my meeting with Mike this afternoon. Mike Cameron is the fourth member of our group friends from university, but I do not see him as often as the others. Mike is a happily married father of one. He married his school sweetheart, Lucy, and appears ridiculously satisfied with life. Lewis was born two years ago and he is a great natured kid, just like his father. Mike is a complete health freak and has been vegetarian since he was twelve years old. He is mostly tea-total, but still enjoys coming to the pub with the rest of us now and again for a catch up as he sips his mineral water in the surroundings of his good friends.

After gaining a first in accounting and finance at Edinburgh University, Mike joined one of the big firms in London, before being transferred back to his native Edinburgh, and has never looked back since. He lives in a large detached house in Ravelston Dykes and Lewis will be following in his father's footsteps by attending Stewarts Melville College. Mike appears to have his life all mapped out before him and, although I find the thought quite frightening, he seems delighted with his lot. This shines through in his positivity every time we meet.

Anyway, Mike and I met for a coffee (one of the large chains, not my Barista's place) and talking to him made me aware of my own situation. So, I have my three point challenge to move my love life closer to order. I didn't confide in Mike to this, however, did disclose my aim to improve my health, drink more water, etc. He immediately adopted his proud father expression, which I imagine appears often. As such, he treated me to dinner at his favourite vegetarian restaurant, which surprising I thoroughly enjoyed.

There was a planned get together tonight for the evening, however, most of the others called off for one reason or another, so I headed home accepting the cancellation. I decided against getting any beer on the way home having enjoyed my healthy dinner, so just picked up a few groceries including another crate of mineral water.

Saturday night television was the usual nonsense that I have the pleasure of missing most weeks, so I ended up playing my guitar for a few hours before bed,

At this rate, the old university band may be heading for a comeback.

Sunday January 9th

I must admit that I am starting to enjoy these evenings, recording my day in this diary. I am trying to write as honestly as possible in case the diary is ever witnessed by another or to remind myself what my life was like at this time when I am older. I do not intend to share these writings (certainly not with Alex), however, no one knows what the future holds. I guess I may have to produce the evidence before the collection of the £100 bet, but I shall hold these notes aloft from a distance.

I should point out, as it is Sunday, and I was far too hung over to think last week, that I am not a religious person. I came from a mixed background and my parents decided to let me choose my own religion should I so wish. As neither of them were regular church goers, I chose to remain without faith. I'm not sure why I have chosen to record this, but it may be relevant in the future – I have no idea.

After a pretty uneventful day (I usually spend the late morning/early afternoon of each Sunday cleaning the flat, washing, ironing, etc.) I went to Dads around 3 o'clock. I enjoy our time together, although we can spend long spells not talking. It never feels uncomfortable and I think this is a mutual feeling. I remember a story Alex once told me about visiting his grandfather in Aberdeen. After driving 4 hours to visit, his grandfather made him a cup of tea then said he better head back before it got too late. I think some of the older generation get used to their own company and often feel as if they want the awkward visits over sooner than the visitor does.

After dinner (always a good traditional Sunday roast) Dad and I played chess for a while. He taught me how to play when I was 8 years old and we have played most Sundays ever since, sometimes only one game as we are now evenly matched in terms of ability. I confessed to playing the piano last Friday and he asked me to play some Beethoven for him. We often spent hours arguing over who was the better composer, I would never stop defending my beloved Mozart, but Beethoven is certainly a close second in my mind. I glanced over to him after a few minutes and could clearly see his eyes start to glisten with tears. I quickly returned to my music and played on longer than I planned. I know for a fact that he noticed me glace at him but little words were passed at the end ('Very good son, lovely'). I think this is a further example of our silent respect for each other.

Monday January 10th

Good news and bad news from work this morning. Darth's mood from Friday was not anything to do with me (what did I tell you.), however, the bad news from London is there is a large restructure of the company in the pipeline and the Edinburgh headquarters is one of the first to be looked at. It is the first time in over 10 years that staff members have been faced with the threat of compulsory redundancy; it has always been managed through 'natural wastage'. Darth is very concerned about her own position given the nature of her role. It is probably the first time I have felt genuinely sorry for her as she has a family and we work fine together, better the devil you know as they say. I am less concerned, funnily enough, about my own position. I can always head back to Dads (the house was transferred to my name when mum died, so technically it is my house) and I have no commitments of real note except the flat which can be rented out in a moments notice. Early indications are that only the management will be affected so at least my team should be safe.

I decided to put in a long shift today and was the last one to leave the office, just after 9 o'clock. With the coffee shop closed when I passed, my thoughts float to an earlier finish tomorrow. A strange lack of appetite means that I took a further stroll along the canal for an hour or so before I headed home. With the weather still dry and my scarf, hat and gloves (the basic requirements of every Edinburgh resident) doing their business, I enjoyed my time watching the wildlife pass me by.

My eyes are now starting to droop so I must bid you farewell, until tomorrow my dear friend.

Tuesday January 11th

Petra, her name is Petra. She is 29 years old and she is Czech (just shows how much I know.). I have not reached stage 3 of my investigation, but as Meat Loaf says – two out of three isn't bad.

I finished work around six and headed into the café. The café itself is a small independently owned place on Bruntsfield Place which I have been visiting for many years now. Petra was working alone and the café was quiet with just two other customers who were both taking advantage if the free Wi-Fi (I expect their coffee cups had been empty for some time). I ordered my coffee and choose a healthy sandwich to save me making dinner when I got home. I quickly took my seat after making some stupid comment about it being a lovely evening (ok, it is still dry, but it is freezing out there). By the time I had finished the two surfers had left and we were alone. I'm not sure how the conversation went exactly, but it went something like this –

Me – 'Hi, err, thanks, err, great coffee as usual'.
Petra – 'You are very welcome'.
Me – 'Oh, and, err, the sandwich, um, very good too'
Petra – 'You are very welcome, again'.
Me – 'Well, err, I guess, I, um, better get home, let you get organised'.

Petra – 'Yes, I guess so'.

Me – 'Thanks, Steve, oh sorry. Steve, err, yes that's my name Steve or Stephen but I like Steve. Steve Hamilton'. (James Bond it was not)

Petra – 'Hi Steve Hamilton, my name is Petra'.

Me ' –Petra, that's really nice. Where is it from? '(Thank God I didn't say where about in Poland.)

Petra – 'It's Czech; I came over from Prague 8 years ago just after my 21st birthday.'

Me – 'Prague, wow, I've never been, but I hear it is lovely'.

Petra – 'For a stag weekend'

She then laughed and I joined her, I often hear Edinburgh described in the same way. I retreated, rather bashfully, quitting when I was only a little behind (before I made a complete arse of myself).

So there you go. I bought myself two bottles of Czech beer on the way home and I am finishing the second as I write this.

I just hope she is single, for now I am completely smitten.

Wednesday January 12th

I met with Linda for dinner this evening which was great, and it was her turn to pay. Linda DeMarco is the final member of the 'Famous Five' friends from university (5 degrees between us and no one can come up with a better term.). Linda is my oldest, and most likely closest, friend. Linda and I have know each other since High School and even dated for a short time back then. We both knew it wouldn't work and broke up before it affected our friendship which was much more important. Since then she has guided and advised me in so much, including relationships, study, careers, etc. I hold her friendship and opinion very close to my heart. That said we also love to take the complete piss out of each other when it is justified.

Linda works as a Senior Asset Manager for a large European Bank in their Edinburgh offices. She often travels down to London and to the Continent which she loves. This did, however, have an impact in her personal life when she split from her long term partner. He wanted her to settle down, get married, have kids, etc. but she was not ready or willing to give up her career. I was fully behind her as she has worked so hard to get where she is within the company and is highly respected in her field. Oh, and her partner was a complete arsehole.

Anyway, healthy eating went out the window as we headed to the Hard Rock Café on George Street. We both love our rock music and with a great burger, good chat and loud music, I was completely at ease. So after the usual catch up, I owned up to my Petra dilemma. She enjoyed teasing me relentlessly about it (and thought I did in fact make an idiot of myself), however, she was at least proud I was making moves in the relationship front. I asked her for advice about how I approach the subject of a date with her (you would think I would know by now, but it has been a while since I last dated). Linda suggested that I just ask her out casually ('But whatever you do, don't ask her out for a coffee'). I suggested taking her to see a movie ('what are you, 16?'), or the theatre to see a play ('what are you, 60?'), so we settled on a meal. 'If she is interested she will accept or make up a good excuse'.

So there we have it, advice sought and delivered from my oldest and dearest friend on the matter. I just hope it turns out better than the last time I offered her advice. 'Sorry I can't come this time, but why not take Wills to the company's drink reception with you…'

Thursday January 13th

'My name is Stephen Hamilton and I am a drug addict' and so begins my monthly meeting.

I started partying quite hard when mum died, just after my first year at university. It started with excessive drinking and the occasional cigarette when I was drunk. I started taking speed to get me through the week at university and cannabis at the weekend to help me relax. The harder I partied, the more drugs I took until it became out of control. It came to a head at the start of my final year when Dad found out. I shouted the vilest of abuse at him and said some unforgivable things. He remained calm throughout and just took the venom I showered him with. I stormed out and after a few days he called and said that when I was ready, I was to come round and speak to him. He was willing to help me in any way he could. I went round that Sunday and broke down completely in front of him as soon as he answered the door (I felt that I could not just walk into the house, I needed to be invited in). We talked for a few hours and I agreed to start going to meetings for drug addicts.

At the start, I went every week, but I was still abusing. My usage was decreasing, but I couldn't go cold turkey. I decide to throw myself in to my study as I knew I had to change my life dramatically and if I failed I would have wasted four years of my life, I took drugs for the last time on the day before my final exams and went out with a whimper rather than with a bang. I got through my finals, securing a 2:1 and graduating with Dad in attendance. I have not looked back since.

It remains the darkest period of my life, but I came through it. I think that is part of the reason I make sure that I visit Dad every Sunday. On top of the many other reasons that I visit, it helps me remember everything he did for me during that period of my life.

Friday January 14th

I write this update at 7 o'clock in the evening on the basis that tonight I am meeting up with the remainder of the 'Famous Five' for a meal and drinks. Having had a couple of awful days at work, I have resigned myself to the fact that I am going to enjoy myself tonight, It is not often that all five of us meet at the same time so it should be a good night.

I suspect tomorrows entry will be written in an element of discomfort…

Saturday January 15th

Never again.

I write this statement as I have said it numerous times today; however, I know that I will enjoy these nights once again, just not for a while. I am conscious that by dealing with my drug addiction, that I must be careful that my alcohol intake does not replace this habit. I made a definite decision that I would keep drinking on a social basis although many addicts give up everything. I gave up smoking at the same time as I thought that this was too closely related to my addiction and I have been completely fine with that. With Edinburgh being a smoke free city in its restaurant and bars, it is a lot easier now than it was at the start.

I must admit that the night was fantastic with everyone being in fine spirits (seriously Steve, what is it with these puns). Alex was delighted to have completed, and been paid for, his commission and insisted on paying for the meal. Wills was also in good form, he always performs best in front of an audience. He was, however, keeping his current partner under wraps but claims that this one is different. Time will tell I guess. Linda appeared tired to me, I think that she has been working harder and longer since she became single again. She did seem to relax as the evening went on and was certainly enjoying the company. As for Mike, he did appear overly quiet for my liking. Yes, he did join in the fun and seemed happy to be with us. He was one of the last to leave (when he is usually the first). I just can't put my finger on it, but I think something is up with him.

I got home around three this morning, but lacked the desire for sleep. I put on the TV and watched some awful movie from the 1980's that was so bad I could not turn it off. I must have finally crawled into bed around six and slept through to three the following afternoon, when I was awoken by the sound of my letterbox rattling. It took me a few minutes to get my bearings, find a t-shirt and get to the door. When I arrived, there was no one at the door and no letters posted. I grabbed my jeans and shoes and went down to the main door. Again, there was no one around and even the street was completely empty. I headed back to the flat for some strong coffee, paracetamol and plain toast. My thoughts returned to the note delivered on the first; however, my head was too sore and tired to contemplate the matter any further.

After a couple of hours on the sofa, I made a small salad for dinner and decided to go for a run. I must have run for forty minutes, but it felt like hours. I wanted to do this to punish myself for continuing to drink longer than I should have, and also to remind myself of the changes I have planned for my life this year,

As long as I live long enough to enjoy them.

Sunday January 16th

I do not concur with the current thinking that 30 is the new 20 or 40 is the new 30 and so on. You are who you are; it is what you do with your life that counts. I am 34 and that is that, not 24, or 44 – 34. You just have to accept what age you are today and what age you become on each birthday.

I had a dream last night that I was standing at a crossroads in some far off location of barren plains (this may have started with my current musical listening choice of Eric Clapton). If I look behind me, I see an image of my past through the heat waves, everything that I have done or neglected, achieved or failed, attended or left. It shows the reasons why I became the person I am today, friend, son, addict, colleague, partner (although not right now). The dream seems to suggest that now is a time to reflect and choose my next path, leaving what has been behind me.

In the dream I can see three roads in front of me. Directly ahead of me is the easy straight road. It has my current job, a wife and children, house and car – what is expected of people in life. To the right is winding road that suggests throwing it all away and starting again. Many twists and turns appear on that road and the destination is uncertain, however, it does appear interesting. The final road to the left is a road which is in immaculate condition. There is a barrier at the start of the road and I can see a number of gates that need to be passed. In the distance I can see a reflection of myself, looking happy and healthy. I can see that this road has the need for me to make the positive changes in my life to get passed each gate. The question is - does it merit the effort? Bloody hell, this was one deep dream.

When I woke from the dream, I had a long look in the mirror as I got myself ready for my weekly visit to see Dad. I think that my party years are starting to catch up with me. I see the beginning of wrinkles around my eyes and dark bags forming underneath. I look tired and I guess I need to get more rest. My dark hair now contains a few strands of gray and my stubble is now mostly ginger and white. I suppose I am still handsome and with some work I could make myself more presentable.

One question remains above all though, why on earth is all this hair spouting out of my ears?

Monday January 17th

Unattached. I must write this again, UNATTACHED. Of course, I am talking about Petra and I couldn't be happier. We have agreed to go for a meal next Saturday (thank you

Linda.). The fact that she accepted my offer makes me feel more relaxed in her presence; however, I have the feeling that there is a lot I need to find out about her. It is like a trial run, nice meal, good wine, a bit of chat to allow us to get to know each other. I don't want to get ahead of myself, however, I feel that this could be the start of something good and just what I need in my life just now (last girlfriend was over 2 years ago now). I have arranged the date so that it can be like speed dating in reverse (I tried it once, truly awful experience) where you actually get time to get to know a person before she turns you down. We agreed to meet at the restaurant at 8 o'clock with nothing planned after, just in case she completely hates me. I chose a nice French restaurant at the Grassmarket – I just hope she turns up.

I called Linda to tell her the news and she spent a full ten minutes teasing me, but truth be told – I loved it. After the teasing and details settled down, I made my concerns about her health be known. She admitted that she has only taken off Christmas Day and New Years Day in the last 3 months and has worked both Saturdays and Sundays within that period. She promised me that was going to take a week off next month, as long as the big contract she was currently working on finished by then.

I decided to clean and restring my guitar tonight. The strings were almost black and have been on the guitar for about four years. I do love the sound of a newly strung guitar. I put on a set of heavy duty Martin strings as I can't afford a Martin guitar just yet. I play a Fender acoustic which does the job and has a nice sound for what I play; however, if I keep playing as much as I have been recently I will need to trade up. I spent around an hour or so playing a few Eric Clapton songs from the 'Unplugged 'album.

A perfect end to what has been a fantastic day.

Tuesday January 18th

I cannot say that I hate work, but I hardly jump out of bed in anticipation of a fun filled day. Darth's mood is dark (very Empire Strikes Back) and she pulls me into her office for a full debrief of the latest Heads of Departments meeting. She admits to being worried about the pending cut backs and this was amplified further when someone from the meeting suggested that we could become a prime takeover target. I am not so sure myself, there is always scaremongering going on and us Scots excel in the 'woe-is-me' stakes. I suggested this to Darth but she just replied with a shrug of her shoulders.

I stopped off for a coffee on the way home, just to see Petra rather than for the caffeine delights. I don't want to stalk her (a restraining order prior to the first date just would not do.) but I just wanted to see her. Everything will change after Saturday, and if it all goes belly up then these times will be no more, so I just want to enjoy them while I can.

I had a quiet night in playing a few tunes and watching some trashy television. I watched some documentary on the current crisis in the National Health Service. I am quite a healthy person and have only been hospital once when I broke my leg jumping from a wall at primary school. I was, to be fair, trying to impress a girl at the time, however, when she heard the bone snap any chance of friendship was dashed. I ended up watching some re-runs of Blackadder Goes Forth which was much more my cup of tea.

Mr Atkinson, sir, you are indeed a genius.

Wednesday January 19th

I hate Facebook, Friends Reunited and I cannot understand why people are fascinated by or interested in 'Tweeting' (even the term is awful.). I only use e-mail at work and have never used Instant Messaging. Why is Social Networking so popular? People are fast losing the art of conversation and the ability to construct a basic sentence. Even when I send a text message, I insist in typing in properly (I cannot abide people who will 'C U L8R'). It is my age? Am I being a grumpy old man before my time? I just have an excessive hatred of this current obsession with Social Networking.

Today's rant has been sparked off by one of my team members, who I have noticed spends more of her time checking her Facebook page on her phone than dealing with her cases. I know I don't run the tightest of ships; however, I also make sure my staff members do the amount of work expected of them. I will tackle the issue at tomorrow's team meeting and see if my usual gentle but firm approach works (to be fair, it usually does).

My other current colleague trait hates in the workplace are as follows –

1 – Tattoos – 4 out of 5
2 – Excessive piercings – 2 out of 5

3 – Ties not worn properly, ties worn too loosely or tied wrongly – 3 out of 3
4 – Poor timekeeping (1 out of 5)

In today's 'Human Rights Gone Mad' culture – I can only address the last one, which has improved recently, but I fully expect will deteriorate in the not too distant future.

Not too long to wait for my big date so I decided to go for a long run this evening, I was out for over an hour and I think the legs will suffer some what tomorrow for it.

I spoke to a few of the guys after I had had a shower and got myself changed. Alex is working on another new script, this one said to be heading for Channel 4 ('Stephen my good man, I'm telling you as sure as eggs are eggs, this one will appeal to the students, academics, philosophers, poets and the greatest of the Great British public'). We will just have to wait and see. Wills was heading out for a 'serious amount of lubrication' (I assume he was referring to alcohol.) and promised to catch up for a game of snooker soon. I also called Mike; however, Lucy answered and confirmed he was not at home. She did not elaborate and ended the call rather quickly. I sense something is afoot, but I just can't put my finger on it.

Thursday January 20th

Rubbish day today. Work was rubbish – I made my feelings known at the meeting, no response. Darth was also in a rubbish mood, but kept mostly out of the way.

I finished at 5, ordered an Indian take away and washed it down with a few beers. Both were too hot and pretty rubbish.

Watched some rubbish on the television and cannot find anything that is not rubbish to write today.

I am going out with Alex tomorrow to see a new play, so hopefully tomorrow will be a better day, and not rubbish.

I have said rubbish too often, don't you think?

Friday January 21st

Alex is my closest male friend and he is also the person I see most often, yet I feel we have very little in common. I always take an interest in his lifestyle and passions, but I don't always share his enthusiasm for them. Opposites attract, so they say, and my mood always seems to pick up when in his company.

I really enjoyed the play. Set in a bar in Glasgow it followed the story of Jake, a one hit wonder movie star who spends his nights downing vodka in a West End bar whilst scribbling masses of notes onto numerous paper napkins, hoping for one last shot at the big time. In true Glaswegian fashion, he drinks himself to death, leaving a shoe box full of his scribbles to his favourite bar tender. As she was studying scriptwriting at university, she goes through the box and discovers an incredible script which allows her to achieve the riches that Jake craved so much.

According to Alex, the play was written by an up and coming writer from Glasgow. Alex spoke at length about his talent and I sensed equal amounts of respect and envy. 'Just need to convince the young man that his future truly lays within the embracing arms of Edinburgh's literary scene' was his only criticism.

Due to his eccentricity, Alex does not let you get much talking done, and to be fair, I enjoyed just listening to him immensely. It was just the tonic for my day yesterday and helped me completely unwind. He has requested full and frank feedback of my 'little outing' tomorrow; however, he refused the urge to tease me, not normally his manner anyway.

And on that note, at exactly two minutes to midnight, I will retire with visions of Petra and an Iron Maiden soundtrack in my head.

Saturday January 22nd

The time is currently 7 o'clock and I have decided to write today's entry early (nothing untoward you understand). One of the rules of the bet with Alex is that I must write everyday and if I don't get back until after midnight, I will have lost (gentlemen's agreement, you see.).

Today I decided to have a clean and de-clutter of the flat. I am usually quite good at keeping the flat tidy, but I do need to get the bleach and cleaning products out a bit more often. Don't get me wrong, it is kept clean; however, any OCD sufferers would have an instant panic attack if I confessed to my cleaning patterns. I grabbed a bag of old clothes and bric-a-brac and took it round to a local charity shop, choosing Oxfam as today's gracious receivers of my goods. I find charity shops fascinating and often wonder what is in the other bags that have been dropped off that day. An old school friend volunteered as part of his Duke of Edinburgh award and said that it was outrageous some of the things people think the can drop off. I always make sure that my items are both presentable and saleable.

I planned to go out for a run this afternoon; however, fearing an untimely accident or injury I decided a walk along the canal was more appropriate. After a mid-afternoon snack I played the guitar for a good 2 hours. The afternoon was filled with Unplugged Grunge music, and I am sure that MTV would have been proud (well, maybe back in 1993.).

So here I sit writing my entry. All dressed up and, for once, somewhere to go.

Sunday January 23rd

The date went really well and Petra and I are firmly on the road to becoming close (I do not like to get ahead of myself.). The meal and restaurant were both a big success and she looked stunning in a long, simple black dress. We talked for a good two hours during the meal and then went to a bar for drinks afterwards. I feel that I must have done most of the talking, but she did confirm that she came over from the Czech Republic five years ago. She has a seven year old son, Lukas, but she did not talk about his father (and I did not ask.).

After drinks, I walked her home to her flat which is just above the coffee shop that she works at. We held hands as we walked up from the Grassmarket and she walked close to me, sheltering herself from the harsh Edinburgh winter's evening. I offered to get a taxi when we left the bar, however, she was happy to walk and I am so glad that she did. I didn't receive an invite in for coffee; however, she did leave me with a most unforgettable kiss and promise to see me again. As first dates go, it was pretty much perfect.

So I'm now off to see Dad, running a bit late but I'm sure he won't mind. I will give him the outlined details of Petra and I am sure he will be happy for me as he has been going on forever about my lack of a 'better half'

'What is the point in living, if you have no one to live it with' is a statement that he often makes. It is a poignant statement, but I know that he has a good group of friends that he lives with and I often wish that he would also find someone special. Although he has never admitted as much, I have my suspicions that he may well have found her already.

Monday January 24th

I took today off work and, when I called her last night, convinced Linda to do the same. I think the temptation of filling her in on all the details of Petra won her over. The real reason, however, is that it is Linda's birthday today and it was as good an excuse as any to get her out of the office for the day.

Linda's main passion out of the office is independent and foreign movies, so I took her for lunch and then for a double bill showing of classic French cinema at the Filmhouse. The plan worked to perfection and I could visually see the tension leave her shoulders as we sat down for dinner at a Mexican restaurant just off George Street.

Linda is delighted that I am so happy at the moment and her current lack of teasing me proves this. We spent most of the meal talking about the old days at school and university. I made a conscious effort not to bring up work as I could see her totally relaxed and knew that having a day away from the job was just what she needed. I even confiscated her Blackberry when we met to ensure there was no lapses.

After the meal I took her home and gave her the present I had bought her. It was a friendship bracelet that had seen in a jeweller on George Street. I thought it was a special gift and with her eyes filling up, I knew Linda thought so as well. I left shortly afterwards so as not to join her.

Tuesday January 25th

I had another pretty uneventful day in the office today. The team seem more or less back to normal. Timekeeping is fine and looks like Facebook updates are being restricted to lunch time and breaks. Darth was in meetings for most of the day so I missed her completely (which is never a bad thing really.)

I finished relatively sharply today and headed straight home to change so that I could take myself out for a run. I was out for about an hour and a half and was dying for the last few miles. Edinburgh looked very peaceful this evening and it reminded me why I love this city so much. It is very compact and when I go out for a run I can cover many different areas of the city in a short space of time. I just wish it was a few (ok many) degrees warmer in temperature.

When it comes to Petra, I currently feel like a young school boy, not really knowing how to handle the situation (ridiculous, I know). It has been quite a while since I last had a serious girlfriend and I am constantly reeling myself in, scared that I will say or do the wrong thing. I have also never dated someone with a child before, however, I guess at the age I am now it shouldn't surprise me. I have always been good around other people's children so I hope that I can meet with Lukas soon, however, I need to let Petra make that decision for herself. I have decided that I will pop in to see her tomorrow for a chat, but I have good reason to do so. With all the excitement of Saturday night, would you believe that I forgot to get her phone number.

Wednesday January 26th

There appears to be something going on at work and I must say that I am quite concerned. Darth pulled me into her office and asked me some questions about 'The Facebook Queen' (her name is actually Samantha and everyone calls her Sam). Sam is quite popular in the office and she is a good worker, with the exception of her mobile phone addiction. Darth would not tell me anything about why she was asking all the questions. She is a bit of a control freak, and enjoys her position of power, so I never really push her for information. Knowing these little things about her makes our working relationship run smoothly, despite what previous managers say about her. She said that I will know more tomorrow and to 'keep things ticking over as normal like you do Steve'.

I finished up around six thirty and headed over to the coffee shop to see Petra. Wills had called off our planned snooker game as he was heading for a 'special night out'. I have no idea what has got into him of late, however, I am sure there is a woman involved. It was quite quiet when I arrived at the coffee shop, so Petra sat with me at a table near the counter. She must have only served a handful of people in the 2 hours I was there and I could not believe it when she kicked me out at nine so she could lock up (time flies in her company). She did, however, agree to my offer of a walk along the canal before she headed home. She told me that her mother lives with her and looks after Lukas when she is working, so she had to give her a quick call first.

It was a still and fresh evening, cold yet comfortable. We walked again holding hands as Petra started to talk to me about her life. She married young and she and her husband moved to Scotland when Lukas was two years old. They initially lived in Glasgow when suddenly her husband was tragically killed when a drunk driver knocked him off his bike when he was coming home from work. She confessed that, until now, she had not even thought about someone else, however, it has been four years since the accident and she knew it was time to move on, although she will never forget. Her hand held mine tightly as she remembered and retold these terrible events. Her mother had come to live with Petra (her father had died a number of years before) when her husband died and they all moved to Edinburgh full time shortly afterwards.

It was so difficult hearing this, but I want to know as much about her as possible and I feel that she felt better telling me this also. I could also sense that with each part of the story told, we were becoming closer if that makes sense? I guess it must have been so very difficult for her to tell me all this, however, she said that she felt she had to tell me this before our relationship went any further. When she finished, I stopped and held her close and tight. It felt like seconds, however, it must have been minutes and I could not seem to find any words to say at that point. I guess my holding her said everything I wanted to say.

When I walked her back to her flat she invited me in, but it was late and I suggested that I could come over on Saturday evening instead. She seemed really pleased at this idea and said that her mother and Lukas would love to meet me (I wonder now as I write this how much she has spoken about me). We swapped numbers and I promised to call her tomorrow night to make the arrangements for Saturday.

And then we kissed.

Thursday January 27th

Darth put me off until tomorrow with regards to Sam, however, I now suspect something pretty serious has happened or is about to happen. I have become quite accurate in my reading of Darth's facial expressions (or the person behind the mask.). The team seem to be pretty up beat, however, I did notice that Sam was quieter than normal and I wonder if she suspects something – or am I just being paranoid?

I called Petra around nine thirty in the evening and we have arranged to spend all of Saturday together. We are going to take Lukas to see a movie in the afternoon and then her mother, Lucie, has invited me for a traditional Czech dinner (I have no idea what that may consist of, but I generally eat anything so I should be fine). According to Petra both Lukas and Lucie are very much looking forward to meeting me and I said that the feeling was very much mutual.

Looking forward to and petrified of in equal measure.

Friday January 28th

Today was a simply awful experience as I had to sack Sam this afternoon. She has been caught selling clients personal details to fund a hidden lavish lifestyle. She has been spending thousands of pounds on designer clothes, shoes and handbags. She has also funded holidays, cars and electrical items through this. Apparently the handbag she took on the last event the team attended cost £2,000 (I think everyone thought it was a fake, bought on her last trip to Ibiza).

I have never even had to formally discipline a staff member before, so it was the most difficult thing I have had to do during my working life. To be fair, she said that it was only a matter of time before she was caught and accepted the sacking without any resistance. Who knows what I would have done had she burst into tears in front of me. The worst part was escorting her off the premises. I just wish Darth had given me some notice instead of keeping it from me.

I informed the staff and let them go for the day (it was around quarter to four). Once they had gone, I cleared out Sam's desk and packed her belongings into a box to send out to her. I just can't believe this has happened and I never suspected a thing.

I met Wills for a drink around six o'clock and, boy, did I need it. We agreed to just have one as he had somewhere to go (no further explanation offered) and I was conscious that I am meeting Petra and family tomorrow.

When I got home, I took my frustration out on my guitar by playing some early Metallica on it. Even played on an acoustic, I was rockin'.

Saturday January 29th

I have just had a simply fantastic day today. Lukas and Lucie were so delightful. Lukas' current passion is Star Wars, so I was completely in my element (as long as we stuck to the original trilogy.). Lucie was very welcoming and the meal she made was delicious.

Lukas went to bed around nine and Petra and I went for a drink. I asked what the meat was that I had had for my main course. She told me it was bulls 'boy bits' and I nearly choked on my beer. She went on to say it was a real delicacy in the Czech Republic and very expensive to buy and how I should be so honoured that she made this dish for me. I said that I was and it was really delicious.

She had me going for a good half an hour until she laughed and said it was Czech meatballs made with beef and a Czech cheese sauce. I am so gullible, but I love that she has a great sense of humour.

Sunday January 30th

Petra is working today so I agreed to meet her again during the week. I have just got off the phone to her; I just want to speak to her all the time. She seems happy to oblige and we can talk for hours. Even Lukas came on the phone for a bit, wanting to talk about which is the best Star Wars movie (Empire, of course).

I went to see Dad as usual and told him everything. Last week I mentioned I had had a date, but left it at that and he did not press me for more. As such, he was happy to get all the details this week. He has given me an open invitation anytime that we want to go over, but I have to make it soon.

Monday January 31st

It felt strange today without Sam and her vacant desk left an emotional void within the team. I count any small blessings and the Monday morning weekend catch up took the edge off the tension. I also have the task of appointing her replacement and Darth wants this done as soon as possible.

When I got home I gave Mike a call. I don't know what triggered it, but I spent much of today thinking about him. He agreed that he wasn't being himself at the moment; however, he did not go into great detail. He did say that work was busy but he was getting on fine. I think that maybe he and Lucy have had a falling out, but they are so close and with Lewis they always give off the persona of a complete and happy family.

I didn't feel tired later on so I threw on my running gear and headed to the Meadows. I decided to run a few circuits because I could stop when I got bored and/or tired. As it turned out, I was running for a good hour and a half before I realised how late it was. As I ran home, I thought once again about the note I received at the start of the year and how no one has claimed responsibility.

I wonder, has the perpetrator forgotten all about it?

Tuesday February 1st

I was awoken at four fifteen this morning by a thump at the door. I grabbed my jeans and a t-shirt and headed to open it. When I got there, no one stood in front of me. Barefooted, I ran down the steps jumping the last five or so as I saw the main door close in front of me. Unfortunately, I landed hard and fell over with a shooting pain running from my foot to my knee. By the time I hobbled to the main door, the person had vanished.

I limped slowly back to my flat and closed the door, locking and bolting it behind me. I turned on the hall light to get my bearings and that is when I noticed the envelope dangling from the letter box. I picked it up and threw it down onto my desk where I situate myself when working from home.

I struggled through to the kitchen to retrieve some ice from the freezer for my ankle (the pain was now restricted to that area only). I wrapped the ice in a towel and headed to the living room and put my foot up on the coffee table with the towel placed on the offending injury. My knee felt fine at this point, so I am hopeful that the ankle is just twisted and no more serious injury was sustained.

I sat there waiting for the pain killers to kick in. Eventually I hobbled over to the desk, grabbing the envelope and returning to the sofa. I noticed that my hands were shaking ever so slightly as I wrestled with the envelope before tearing it open, retrieving the note inside. It was in the same format as the last note, only this time it was more threatening.

'I hope you enjoyed the month of January, as your final countdown has now begun.'

Wednesday February 2nd

I called Darth to arrange a few days holiday which she was happy to agree to, given I had to carry over two weeks extra unused holiday from last year. I'm not one to call in sick and I am happy to use up some of my leave anyway. Nevertheless, my ankle feels so much better now with little pain or swelling. It could be that I just tweaked it whilst running and jumping a few too many stairs was enough to cause a bit of pain.

That is what I said to Petra when I called her this morning before her shift started. I decided to leave out the part about the evil postman. In the cold light of day, I once again suspect that this is a hoax. The notes are not giving much away; however, I still suspect one of the guys is responsible for all of this (I can say 'guys' because Linda is far too mature to join in on our childish pranks).

I spent most of today with my ankle raised and glued to the television. I bought a DVD box set of Alfred Hitchcock movies a while back, so I thought I would take advantage and open it up and put on some movies. Over the course of the day, I ended up watching three of them. Lunch comprised of toast and tuna whereas pizza was duly delivered to cover dinner.

If the ankle holds up, I may attempt a wander down for a coffee tomorrow evening. I'm sure there will be more than just the caffeine to cheer me up.

Thursday February 3rd

The ankle is feeling pretty good and there is very little swelling left now. I suspect that this injury could be the ankle equivalent of 'Man Flu'. That stated, I did manage another two Hitchcock movies this afternoon and the local Chinese restaurant kindly delivered some Sweet and Sour chicken for my dinner. I don't think I will be running again for a week or so, but I better get some proper food in or I will be adding a stone or so extra weight onto the ankle when I do put the running shoes back on.

I promised Wills last night we would be back at the snooker hall within a fortnight when I called him. I told him about the ankle, but again missed out the part about the note. He is high on my suspect list; however, he showed little interest in how it happened and was more insistent that we meet up next week for snooker. He stated that he has something he needs to speak to me about ('but it has to be face to face, mate'). Will his secret romance finally be set for a revealing?

The ankle was just about able to make it to the coffee shop to meet with Petra. I arrived an hour or so before her shift ended and sat in my (now regular) table nearest to the counter. I hobbled over from the door and she made a great fuss over my injury, which I had strapped up for effect and to my great fault – I lapped up all the attention.

We agreed to meet on Saturday at which point she told me that she has a surprise for me. I declined the offer to pop up to her flat as I didn't want to disturb the family, so I kissed her goodnight ('dobrou noc') and made my way, slowly and with effort, back home.

Friday February 4th

After finishing another two Hitchcock films, I decided to give the flat a bit of tidy today. The ankle is now taking my weight with little complaint, so I decided to pop out to the local supermarket to buy some healthy supplies. I managed to make a rather tasty Chicken Caesar Salad (if I say so myself) and a fruit salad to follow.

Having passed up an invite to the pub, I found myself craving a cold beer, however, due to recent feastings I decided to buy a few alcohol free bottles. Although not a patch on the real thing, it served both palette and conscience well.

Saturday February 5th

Petra has just awoken me with a phone call and it is now just after eight o'clock. She wants me to arrive at her flat at ten o'clock when breakfast will be served. She said I will be out late, so I decided to write today's entry early to ensure I fulfil my one a day promise to Alex.

I feel I might have to start carrying it around with me.

Sunday February 6th

The time is a quarter to midnight and I am writing this with fifteen minutes to spare. I think with the amount I have to write tonight that I will still be going on into tomorrow (does that count for tomorrow's entry also? – No, I think I will stick to the one each and every day rule as I need to win this bet fair and square.).

I arrived at Petra's flat just after ten yesterday morning and she was there alone. It transpired that her aunt and uncle, who are currently over visiting from the Czech Republic and have rented a cottage near Loch Lomond, were entertaining both Lucie and Lukas for the weekend there. They arrived on Friday and spent the day in Edinburgh (Petra took the day off work to be with them) and they all left for the cottage on Friday evening.

Breakfast awaited my arrival and I tucked into a Continental and Cooked breakfast doubler. After helping with the washing up, we headed to the Filmhouse cinema as she had ordered tickets for a Mexican movie that was having a one off showing. It turned out to be an inspired choice for it was one the best movies I have seen in years (Petra agreed).

As a way of celebration I suggested that we eat Mexican for dinner (our overly large breakfast had seen us bypass lunch and popcorn). We headed off for a walk through the Grassmarket before heading over the Royal Mile and down through Princes Street gardens. After negotiating our way through the tourists and tram works of Princes Street we got a table at a small Mexican restaurant just off George Street. We ordered just after five o'clock at which time the restaurant was still quite quiet for a Saturday, however, it started to fill up as we polished off dessert.

I suggested we head to a bar for a few drinks, however, Petra suggested she would rather pick up a bottle of wine and head back to the flat. She said that the flat was rarely empty and she wanted to enjoy a quiet evening relaxing with me.

After taking an age to choose a wine, I settled for a white Boudreaux and red Chianti. I should point out at this point that I am utterly hopeless at this most simplest of tasks. I use a tried and tested, self taught method as follows

1 – Choose a bottle that is pretty to look at.
2 – The bottle must have a cork – never screw top.
3 – Never read the description of the wine written on the label.
4 – Never choose a wine out with the EU
5 – If white, choose French.
6 – If red, choose Italian

We reached Petra's flat around eight o'clock just as the rain started pouring down. Petra threw a hand towel at me as I walked through the front door then, whilst rubbing her own hair with another towel, set about lighting candles in the sitting room. I headed for the kitchen to put the white wine in the fridge and collect some glasses and a corkscrew (both of which were sitting on the counter top and I do not recall them being there earlier when I was washing the dishes).

Petra had put on some music and I was impressed to hear an early Europe album. ('They were very popular in the Czech Republic when I was at school. I think mum still has my Joey Tempest poster at home for me.') She flashed that wonderful smile of hers as she spoke and when she finished I grabbed her and kissed her like it was the first time, but without the nerves.

We spent the next few hours talking about our lives, Petra about growing up in the Czech Republic and me about my mother's death. I found it so easy to open up and I told her about my drug addiction. She seemed shocked at first, but very supportive. Having been clean now for nearly ten years I hope there will never be a problem again, but I keep going to my meetings each month even just to serve as a reminder of my past.

After the red wine was finished, I stood up to collect the white from the fridge, but Petra stopped me suggesting that we leave it for another day. I started to say something about better not to mix your grapes and hangovers as Petra took my hand and led me out of the living room. Her bedroom was small and I noticed as we passed the main bedroom that her mother and Lukas shared that room. There was a candle lit by the bed, which I don't remember her lighting (must have been done at my last toilet trip). We stood at the bottom of her bed and she started kissing me.

I refuse to write further about the rest of the evening, except to record that it was perfect. It was good thinking of me keeping the writing going like I did. I thought I may have been home late, however, I did not think I would not be home at all.

This morning we lay in bed until noon. I popped out of the flat for breakfast and newspapers, with Petra insisting that we utilise both in bed. I was not going to argue. After Petra put a call into Lucie and Lukas she joined me as I headed home to get changed and have a shower.

I thought that it was time that Dad and Petra were introduced to one another so we headed over together. Dad was very hospitable and they seemed to hit it off straight away. Petra was keen to find out as much as possible and Dad obliged by telling some of my most embarrassing stories of my life. It was all done in perfectly good humour.

After dinner, Petra asked me to play piano to her, so I played some Beethoven (to keep Dad happy) and Mozart. I then started playing some Jazz and Blues for some strange reason; however, it all went down well.

Petra and I left at around seven o'clock to get back for Lucie and Lukas. We arrived just before they got home and Lukas was delighted to see me. I had to decline the offer of a Star Wars movie (he has school tomorrow.), but accepted his request to read a bedtime story. I stayed for a coffee with Lucie (who confirmed that she had a wonderful time, despite the weather).

As I bid Lucie a good night, Petra walked me down to the main door. The rain had suddenly started, and with venom. I lingered at the doorway until Petra pushed me out on to the pavement, soaking me through in an instance. When I had gathered my composure, and wiped the rain from my eyes, she stood in front of me equally drenched and awaiting her goodnight kiss, for which I duly obliged.

Monday February 7th

After my action filled weekend, today turned out to be pretty much uneventful. I decided to work on to around nine o'clock as I had a fair amount to catch up on, and my e-mail inbox was bursting at the seams.

Darth welcomed me back with a demand to have Sam's job advertised internally by the end of the day. As such, much of the day was spent negotiating with the Human Resources department about job specification, advert wording, etc. I did manage to get the advert up (with Darth's approval none the less.) by the end of the day as required. A closing date of next Monday confirmed her eagerness to get this matter concluded pronto.

I just worry about the calibre of the applicants.

Tuesday February 8th

I called Wills after work to confirm our snooker arrangements for tomorrow night. I told him all about Petra and he is delighted for me, but he was a bit light on the teasing for a change. He wants to meet up earlier than usual, so it could be a trip to Burger King for dinner tomorrow, or as we say in Edinburgh, Burger King for tea. In Edinburgh breakfast is breakfast, lunch is dinner and dinner/supper is tea. I tend to stick to breakfast, lunch and dinner as that is how I was brought up. 'Tea is a drink not a meal' was often shouted out in our house when anyone made a verbal error.

I called Petra after I had spoken to Wills and we talked for a good hour or so. I'm just so happy at the moment and we have agreed to meet up on Thursday after work.

Wednesday February 9th

I finished work at six o'clock and stopped off at Burger King before meeting Wills just before seven. We duly purchased our table and beers and headed over to 'rack up'. Once I broke off, Wills opened his heart to me in a way I have never seen him react before (sorry if this is getting a bit Jane Austin).

It transpires that Wills has been dating a student he met at a Christmas party last year. Apparently, she is funny, charming, and exceptionally beautiful. He confided that he is just incredibly happy in her company. His problem is that she is only twenty two years old. With Wills having turned thirty five at the end of last year, he is concerned about the thirteen year gap.

They have been dating casually since the party, but now she wants them to become a 'proper couple'. Wills is torn and I can tell that he is very fond of her. I suggested that if he feels that way about her, he should just go with it. He confessed that sometimes it feels odd, just not right, but other times he has never felt better. I'm not the best at relationship advice, and admitted as much to him, so I suspect that Linda will be getting a call soon.

This matter is obviously playing deeply on his mind, as I won the snooker match five frames to nil.

Thursday February 10th

I had another late one at work, so it was straight for a coffee on the way home. Petra made me up a sandwich with some leftovers before closing up the café at nine. She suggested a short walk so we headed around Tollcross and up and over the Royal Mile before heading home (Lucie had texted to say that Lukas was fast asleep and not to hurry home).

Petra told me that they are all going over to the Czech Republic for five days next week (Monday to Friday) for a family get together. It was all arranged last minute and she seemed sad to be going. We agreed to spend the weekend together before they head off early Monday morning.

After bidding her, and Lucie, a goodnight I walked home in a bit of a sulk. With some depressing Pink Floyd currently playing in the background, I cannot believe how miserable I am feeling.

And it is only going away for five days.

Friday February 11th

After work I met up with Alex, Wills and Linda for drinks. Most of the evening was dedicated to teasing me about Petra, but it was the usual good natured banter. Wills is keen to meet her; Alex thought he had other reasons for this. Linda wants to fill her in on my past and warn her (although I'm not sure of what exactly.). Alex wants to discuss an early Twentieth Century Czech novelist and playwright, although I have no idea who he was referring to.

Wills joined me at the bar when it was my turn to buy the drinks and thanked me for keeping quiet about his current relationship. I told him that the others would soon work out that something was happening, but I remain loyal to his confidence. He is meeting up with her this weekend and agreed to call me on Monday.

I left the bar around nine o'clock and headed home. Linda has taken next week off so we agreed to spend some time together. I think I will use up some more holidays myself. I called Petra to make arrangements for the weekend. I've to come for lunch tomorrow at twelve o'clock and we will take things from there.

I also called Mike as, although he is not out often, I thought he might have turned up tonight at the pub. He said that Lewis had been feeling ill and wanted to stay with him. We spoke for a while and I told him all about Petra and his mood seemed to lighten. He then started teasing me about how 'I used to play the field, now I was playing a whole Continent'. I made some sort of reference of being a fair bit behind Wills in this regard. I could hear Lucy shouting for him in the background and he ended the call a little abruptly.

I will give him a call next week and arrange to meet up.

Saturday February 12th

I had another fine day with Petra today. I arrived at her flat for lunch as planned we all sat down together. Petra and I took Lukas to the Meadows where he spent most of the time running around over the vast fields. Lukas loves the outdoors and runs everywhere. I was exhausted just watching him.

I decided to take Petra, Lukas and Lucie for dinner and headed for a Chinese Restaurant on Lothian Road. Lukas just wanted some fried rice and I was worried that I had chosen wrongly, but then he started eating from everyone else's plate. When we were finished he told me that it was the best meal he had ever had, before adding 'after last year's Christmas dinner' (with a worried glance in Lucie's direction).

After coffee in Petra's flat, I headed home happy and Petra and Lukas agreeing to come round tomorrow. I called Dad to confirm that there would be three for dinner tomorrow and set my alarm for ten o'clock tomorrow morning.

That will give me two hours of tidying before they are due to arrive.

Sunday February 13th

I have had a great day today with Petra and Lukas. After cleaning the flat frantically (although to be fair, it was not too bad), I made them both some lunch for when they arrived. Over lunch, I gave Petra a book as an early Valentines Day present. I chose Mark Haddon's 'The Curious Incident of the Dog in the Night-Time'. Although not the most romantic of choices, it is a book that I really enjoyed reading (although it was a while ago). To my surprise, Petra also bought me a book for the same reason. It is a book by Petra Hulova called 'Through Frosted Glass'. It looks a beautiful book; however, the book is in Czech. Petra has, however, promised to read it to me in English.

Dad seemed to have a great time and I could see that he enjoyed having Lukas round. I played some piano and even taught Lukas some. He enjoyed Mozart very much, so I can see he has great taste (much to the annoyance of Dad.).

We took Lukas home after dinner as they have an early flight, so I had the evening to myself. I decided to watch another Hitchcock film from the box set to pass the time, but it is only nine o'clock and it's finished already.

I guess it is an early night for me then.

Monday February 14th

Petra called me at five o'clock this morning from the airport,
just before she boarded the plane. I'm not a great morning
person, but with an early night last night and the gesture of the
call, I was not for complaining.

I headed into work early as I have decided to take Wednesday,
Thursday and Friday off. Work was quite uneventful, but I did
have the chance to look through some of the applications for
the job. The closing date is today, so I will review the final
ones tomorrow before selecting those for interview. I have
scored off next Monday for the interviews and I will get them
all done on the one day.

After work, I headed to my monthly meeting. I feel a lot more
positive now, both about my life and my addiction. Although I
have not touched drugs for nearly ten years, I am and will
always be an addict. I really enjoyed my meeting today,
certainly more that I usually do. I guess having my life going
in the right direction helps and hopefully I can inspire others,
especially those who have only recently started attending.

When I got home, I called Wills for an update on his current
dilemma. He said that he had had a great time over the
weekend, but has still not decided what to do. I am at a loss,
so I suggested he call Linda.

When I came off the phone, my mind wandered once again to
the notes that I have received. It has now been a month and a
half and still no one has come forward to accept
responsibility. I must admit, I am starting to feel a little
uncomfortable, but I still think it will be a hoax. Wills is my

prime suspect, however, it could be with his current problems he has forgotten all about it.

Or is this happening for real?

Tuesday February 15th

This morning at work I have reviewed nine applications in total, four of which were thrown out straight away. They were simply appalling attempts. I am convinced that text speak, Facebook, Twitter, et al are to blame but I have ranted on this subject already in these pages. Of the five remaining, two were definite interviews and I selected two more after toiling. I made the decision to interview four and have arranged the interviews for next Monday, having booked a Human Resources representative for the day. Darth seemed content with proceeding.

I called Linda and arranged to meet up on Thursday for the day. She has been enjoying the week off, but did confess to dealing with some e-mails (much to my annoyance).

When I got home, I decided to head out for a gentle run. It's the first time since the ankle incident so I took it very slowly. The ankle held up well, but I was exhausted after thirty minutes, so called it a day,

Use it or lose it I guess.

Wednesday February 16th

I had an enjoyable day to myself today, messing around the flat, having a clear out, getting shopping in, watching some television, etc. It is strange sometimes how time flies by and you feel as if you have pottering about for only an hour, when three or four have actually passed.

I met Wills for snooker and he was in fine form. He had spoken to Linda earlier in the day about his ongoing relationship issue. Although she did not let pass the opportunity for some pretty severe ribbing, she agreed with me. If they are both happy, just run with it and see what happens. It seems that we are to meet her in the not too distant future, none the less.

Speaking to Linda certainly worked wonders on his snooker ability, for it was my turn for a five nil beating.

Thursday February 17th

I spent the day in Edinburgh with Linda today. We had a wander round the shops with her forcing me to buy some new clothes and shoes. I hate this kind of shopping and always have. To me, they are functional rather than fashionable, but in truth Linda does pick well.

We had a good laugh at Wills' expense, but we are both happy for him (and a little relieved). Linda wanted to know everything about Petra and her family. She is looking forward to meeting her and I suggested that they would like each other (then I made some terrible joke about her Czech Mate.).

I went for another run this evening despite the truly dreadful weather. It poured from the heavens all evening (I wonder what Atheists would say?). I pushed myself for an hour and felt better for it.

I'm not sure how I will feel in the morning though.

Friday February 18th

Petra is due back today. She called me from Prague airport at dinner time and her flight is due in at 11:45. I suggested that I could meet them, but she said not to bother as they will all be tired and she would rather call me tomorrow.

I had lunch at Linda's house today and pressed her on her own love life situation (anything to stop the endless questions about Petra and me.). She confessed that she was going on a date tonight, but would not say anymore than that. I continued to press her for more information, I even pushed, pulled and yanked but she was not for saying anymore on the subject.

Don't you just hate it when that happens?

Saturday February 19th

It was wonderful to see Petra again and I felt every minute of the five days she was away. It transpires that they had a great time, but felt that Lukas had to work on his Czech accent.

I could tell that Petra was tired from the trip and I think she must have crammed a lot of family visits into the five days. The rain was relentless today, so we spent the day at Petra's flat. Lukas was sleeping by seven o'clock and Lucie went to bed at nine. Petra and I started to watch a movie; however, she never lasted the first hour. I carried her to her room and kissed her goodnight before heading home glad to have been in her company again.

Sunday February 20th

Petra called me to thank me for getting her to bed and apologised for falling asleep on me. She feels much better today after having a long lie in, but suggested that she would rather just stay in by herself today.

I headed over to Dads earlier than normal and let myself in as I thought Dad would still be at the bowling club. I walked into a bit of a shock, when I found him having tea and sandwiches with a 'lady friend' who I may have seen around the bowling club before. Dad had an embarrassed look about him, similar to that of a teenage boy caught with his first girlfriend. His friend introduced herself as Mary, before saying that she was just leaving. I sat by the piano as Dad saw her to the door to say his goodbyes. When he returned a few minutes later I started playing 'All you need is love' and, fortunately, he saw the funny side.

He was just as secretive as Linda about his new 'friend', but I can tell that he is happy to have company which is just great. After dinner, he thrashed me at chess and I can see that his game had the same influence as Wills' snooker the other night.

If this continues, I will have to find another hobby.

Monday February 21st

Interview day today and I will rename the candidates (to protect the guilty) as follows –

1 – Weegie Willie
2 – Liar Louise

3 – Average Joe
4 – Successful Sue

Willie was first up, 28 years old just moved over from Glasgow. Now, before I start I must make one thing clear. I do not agree with the great East West divide of my country and I love both Edinburgh and Glasgow. That stated the 40 or 50 miles separating the two cities could be another continent. Willie's CV was fine and he obviously put in effort for his application. I suspect that nerves got the better of him on the day as he spent the whole interview scratching at his armpits. He also arrived with a well known Scottish tabloid newspaper which I could see poking out of the inside pocket of his, oversized, suit jacket. Verdict – Err, no.

Second up was Louise. Now Louise, 32 from Livingston, was very well presented and submitted an excellent application. The interview went well and she gave some good answers. I noticed in her application she stated that her interests included Classical Music. At the end of the interview, I asked her who her favourite composers were and what pieces she enjoyed most, and this is where it went all wrong. She obviously knew very little and at one point she stated that she loved all the German composers especially Wagner (said with a W not a V), Bach, Mozart (half right) and Strauss (Austrian).Verdict – Close, but no cigar.

After lunch I had the 'Pleasure' of meeting Joe, 23 from Broxburn. Joe also presented a good application and CV. It was going pretty well until I asked about his degree. He replied something like –

' I got a 2:2, which was OK, but my results always tend to be pretty average, but I was happy just to pass in the end, err, you know what university is like'.
Verdict – Less than average chance of getting the job.

Finally, we had Sue, 28 from Stockbridge in Edinburgh. Sue had submitted the best application and her CV was the most impressive. She gave the best interview despite the over usage of the word success (and similar).
'After I successfully passed my degree…., I undertook this project which was a great success…., I always aim to succeed in everything I do…, etc.'
At one point, I was ready to hit her over her head with a Thesaurus. Verdict – Successful candidate.

So, Sam will be replaced by Sue and will start next Monday. I just hope she does not spend all her time on Facebook.

Tuesday February 22nd

Darth is satisfied with the job of replacing Sam and thanked me for getting it all arranged. She seemed in a good mood today, which is always of a concern with her.

Petra is working tonight and I agreed to meet up with her later in the week. She said that she has a lot to get done around the flat, so we agreed to catch up later.

My phone rang around nine thirty this evening and I ran to answer it having just came out of the shower (I managed another run tonight and it is slowly coming back). It was Mike and he said that Lucy was out with friends for the evening and Lewis was fast asleep. At that point he started to open up and said that he has been having marriage problems for over a year now. Lucy was constantly picking fights with him, but until recently she had been retaining the 'Happy Couple' outlook. She was now not hiding her unhappiness and it all came to a head at a recent business function they attended together. Apparently, Lucy embarrassed Mike in front of a very important client. He was able to save that professional relationship; however, it had severely wounded his marriage.

I asked if they had considered marriage counselling, however, he said that Lucy was not interested. He now thinks that she has been having an affair for the last year. It sounded to me that he has already lost hope. I suggested that maybe he needed a night out and asked if he fancied meeting up with everyone on Friday night. This seemed to pick him up and he thought it would be just what he needed.

I think it is time for Petra to meet everyone too.

Wednesday February 23rd

Work passed with no great events and I headed home early to get some food and to get changed for the snooker session. I made a few calls before I left and Linda, Alex and Petra are all available for Friday. When I met Wills, he also agreed to meet and said he would also bring along Kylie (oh yes, that is really her name.)

Wills was once again in good form, however, I think he is a little apprehensive about bringing Kylie along on Friday. He was being all confident and butch about it, however, I have known him too long to be fooled. It may have affected his snooker also, as I sneaked a 3-2 win in the end.

Thursday February 24th

Another dull day in the office, however, the team meeting was good fun. I announced the arrival of Sue for Monday coming and spent the entire meeting diverting all their questions about her. They will just have to wait and see for themselves.

Petra was working again tonight, but I stopped for a coffee and a chat on the way home. The café was quite quiet so we had a good talk about life in general. She is very much looking forward to meeting everyone tomorrow night but she asked me to tell her more about those who were coming.

I think it went something like –

Alex – my closest friend loves the arts but can be overly eccentric at times (although I love this about him).
Mike – quiet one, may not talk much as he is having some personal issues at the moment.
Linda – the sane one and good friend. She wants to spill all the beans about me, but I will get my own back on her.
Wills – Jack has not quite grown up yet and accepted that he graduated ten years ago.
Kylie – Wills' new girlfriend, yes that is her name, yes I think it was after Miss Minogue and yes, she is that young (but Wills is sensitive, so best not to mention it.).

Friday February 25th

It is the afternoon before the evening after and I am just about to leave the flat to pick up Petra. She told me earlier when I called her that she is really excited about meeting everyone tonight and I hope that she is not disappointed. I thought I would write today's entry before I left, just in case it turns out to be a late evening.

I just hope that it is not overly eventful.

Saturday February 26th

What a night it turned out to be.

I picked up Petra and we went for a pre-meeting drink. She wanted some more information about everyone before we arrived, so I filled her in the best I could. She has made arrangements with Lucie for a late night and asked if she could spend the night at mine, so that was an unexpected bonus (good job I had a tidy of the flat before I left.).

We arrived at the pub and everyone was there. I introduced Petra to each in turn before we were both introduced to Kylie. We were all sat at a round table and I strategically planned our seating so that Petra sat next to Linda and I sat next to Alex. Mike was sitting between Alex and Wills, leaving Kylie between Wills and Linda.

Kylie is a very attractive girl, but came across as a little immature, even for her age. Wills looked happy and relaxed in her company, so that was fine for me. That said it nearly went terribly wrong when she asked why we called Jack 'Wills'.

'Because of Jack Wills' he reassured her.

She still looked confused, and I guess Wills will set the record straight later. At that point Alex leaned over to me and whispered, '…and that young man often finds himself all over students'. I nearly fell off my chair and had to head straight off to the bar as I stifled my laughter. I think that we got away with it, but only just.

Mike joined me at the bar and thanked me for listening to all his woes the other night. He asked me for discretion as he was not up for telling the others at this stage. I assured him I was 'discretion itself' in my best Poirot accent. To be truthful, I felt complimented that he chose to discuss the matter with me in the first place.

When I returned to the table, I caught Linda telling an extremely embarrassing story about my youth (no need to repeat this on these pages). I got my own back, however, before asking her how her date went. It was then her turn to feel embarrassed, before admitting that it was a complete disaster. Due to the large amount of Gin and Tonics she had consumed at that point, she confessed that it had been an internet date. 'First one and very much the last one.' she confirmed. 'The photo looked like Brad Pitt, but the reality was more like Bradley Walsh.'

Alex confirmed that he has been snowed under with his work (although we do not often get to see the fruits of his labour.). He confirmed that he has finished his screenplay for the short film which is 'bound of Cannes' and tinkering with his 'Channel Four project'. He really is a man of mystery at times. He also has another painting commissioned, but was keeping tight lipped on that front.

The evening finished at just after midnight and Petra and I headed back to the flat. Petra was a little uneasy on her feet, but she did state that she had had a great time and she and Linda were meeting up again during the week.

I made coffee when we got in and we decided to take them to bed with us, but in the morning they were lying on the bedside table, cold and untouched.

Sunday February 27th

Yesterday, Petra and I had a lazy morning and sorted out our hangovers before heading down to get Lukas. Petra does not drink often, so she confessed it was a bit of a treat for her and it was good to see her being so relaxed.

We took Lukas to the cinema then headed out for dinner. Lucie was not feeling well, so she decided to just stay at the flat. After dinner, we headed back to my flat and watched some television before heading back to Petra's to get Lukas to bed.

Today the three of us headed to Dads for dinner (Lucie declined the invite and was having a day in bed). I took the opportunity to grill Dad on his new friend which was much to my pleasure. He tried to argue that he was too old for a girlfriend; however, I can tell that Mary is special to him. I suggested that he should invite her for dinner next Sunday so we can get a proper chance to meet.

Ah, I sense that there is life in the old dog yet.

Monday February 28th

Today was the day of Sue. I was responsible for getting her settled in and introduced to the team. By the afternoon she seemed to relax more and turned into a completely different person to the one I interviewed (for the better I must add, and she never said success once.). I took her along to meet Darth, who gave her a bit of a grilling but she handled herself well. I am confident that she will be very successful in the role (Oh crap she's got me started.)

I had a lazy evening this evening and settled down to watch another Hitchcock (not many left now.). I called Petra before it started and she had just been on the phone to Linda, so they are meeting up tomorrow night.

Czech mate indeed.

Tuesday March 1st

It happened again, another note only this time it was more sinister. It came in the same format as before and must have been delivered during the night. This one says –

'I've been watching you. Don't get too used to having fun, for unpleasant things are soon to happen'.

I'm starting to think that it is more than just a hoax now, but I don't think the police would be interested at this time or take it too seriously for that matter. I think I might approach Alex on the issue as I am convinced that he is not responsible, it is just not his style.

I put the note with the others and headed off to work. With everything else that is going on in my life at present, I had forgotten all about the notes and did not even realise that they have all been delivered on the first of the month. This one though is hitting a nerve more that the others and I found my mind was wandering to it throughout the day today. I'm not sure whether it is the content of this note, or the fact that my relationship with Petra is taking off at the same time.

On a more positive note, Sue is settling in well and seems to have picked up on the role well. I have one of the other girls in the team sitting with her this week to show her the ropes, but early feedback is very good.

As Petra and Linda were out together tonight, I had another evening with Mr Hitchcock. Dial M for Murder maybe was not the best choice under the current circumstances though.

Wednesday March 2nd

Darth is down in London for the rest of this week to attend a series of meetings. She muttered something about a 'Do or Die' meeting being scheduled for Friday morning. She did not appear to be in a mood to elaborate on the matter, and I didn't push her for more information (I learned early that she will tell me when she is ready). Sue continues to do well and I caught up with her this afternoon to see how she was feeling and settling in. The feedback from her, at the moment at least, is very positive.

I decided to collect a coffee to go on the way home and Petra said that she had had a wonderful time with Linda. Apparently they are planning a shopping trip to Glasgow in the coming weeks. I asked what was wrong with Edinburgh but apparently I am a typical man who knows nothing about this.

Snooker was cancelled tonight as Wills was going out with Kylie and some of her friends to see a movie; I gathered from the tone of his voice he was a little apprehensive. I made my way home to prepare a healthy salad for dinner. Once it had digested, I headed out for a run, hoping I had left sufficient time that I would not be seeing it again. I headed back up to the Meadows and ran laps for an hour or so. I felt good and the salad was safe. I love the Meadows and, even in the pitch dark of night time, it is magical.

Thursday March 3rd

It turned out to be a busy old day in the office today. With Darth away, I seemed to get involved in endless (and pointless) meetings throughout the day. I wonder if the real reason for the recent global economic crisis is down to these types of meetings and the everlasting time people spend creating, printing, colour-coding, discussing and eventually binning spreadsheets. I heard that in Japan businesses have started having 'Standing Up' meetings in a bid to save time. I think these would be useful in our office where the overweight, overpaid directors (who attend meetings only to hear the sound of their own voice) might just get on with some work.

Or will they just request more bloody spreadsheets.

Friday March 4th

Petra is working tonight, so I am heading out with Alex tonight. He is meeting up with an old friend who also happens to be heavily involved (and able to heavily influence) at the Edinburgh Film Festival. Alex is looking to plug a short film that he has just finished writing and has a production company interested in filming should he get a buy in from the EFF ('not that it needs to be sold by me Stephen. The writing sells itself…'). At last I may get to hear about one of his projects during the work in progress stage.

I called Mike for a chat and suggested that he could come over one night next week. He thought that this was a great idea as it would get him out of the house for a bit. It appears that things are not improving and he said that he is finding any excuse to get out of the house once Lewis is sleeping.

I also called Wills on his mobile to see how Wednesday night went, but it must have been switched off as it went straight to voice mail. This, I must admit, is very unusual for Wills as he keeps his phone on as often as he wears those ridiculous sunglasses.

Unless, of course, he was in the middle of something…

Saturday March 5th

Indeed he was.

He called me this morning to say that he had been out with Kylie and they had nipped over to his flat before heading out to a night club. He said that he was very drunk by the time he got home, but he remembered that it was around four o'clock this morning. He arrived home and admitted that he lost sight of Kylie around two and has no idea what happened to her (and she's not answering her mobile). What I do not understand about this is how can he call me at a half past ten on the morning after and sound so unaffected by any signs of a hangover.

The night on Wednesday went well apparently, however, that was more because the movie was good and it provided a diversion away from her group of friends. I don't think Kylie was the only immature one in the crowd.

The night last night with Alex was great fun, but that was more down to seeing Alex on his absolutely best form. As soon as I saw that he turned up wearing a purple velvet smoking jacket, a Paisley Pattern cravat and beige corduroys, I knew we were in for a good night. I swear he took his eccentricity to a whole new level. The trick worked however as he got the buy in from his friend, who had trouble stopping reading from the script he was presented with throughout the dinner. By the time dinner was over, Alex had ordered a bottle of Champagne; he has class that boy (which matches his confidence and sheer cheek.).

The story is set in 1920's Edinburgh and is a tale of a successful businessman who has lost the majority of his money on a deal gone wrong. He is recently married and has a first child on the way and he is determined not to admit the loss of his fortune. The story follows his deception towards his family and friends that all is well in his business, whereas in reality he has turned to underground crime to fund his lifestyle. Needless to say, however, Alex stopped short of giving me a copy of the script or telling me how the story unfolds.

I spent the day with Petra and Lukas having headed down to their flat after lunchtime and we all went out for a walk. She said that she is worried about her mum as she is still feeling unwell. Apparently she refuses to see a doctor (does not want to waste their time.) and she has been going to her bed early most nights. I tried to reassure her as best I could, and it may well just be one of the many bugs that surround this city at this time of year.

We decided to head back to mine for dinner so not to disturb Lucie; however, when we got there the cupboards were bare. Excellent reason to call out for pizza I thought.

Sunday March 6th

I took Petra and Lukas over to Dads today and, to my pleasant surprise, Mary was there when we arrived. We had a good chat about all manner of things as Dad prepared dinner and she is really nice. I am so happy for Dad that he has some good company and I can see that it is making a difference for him.

I was forced once more onto the piano stool after dinner and played some Beethoven for Dad, some Tchaikovsky for Mary, some classic rock for Petra and Coldplay for Lukas. After that we left Dads to get Lukas home, but Mary stayed on. We said our goodnights and I aimed a subtle wink at Dad.

I helped Petra get Lukas into bed and had a chat with Lucie before she retreated also. I can see that she is far from 100% and she certainly looked tired. I can also see the worry on Petra's face but it was clear she didn't want to talk about it.

We snuggled up on the sofa with the television providing a background distraction. Petra talked some more about the Czech Republic and I sense that she misses it somewhat, although, she said she has no plans to return to stay. I suggested that we should all go over sometime, even if it was just for a long weekend as I am keen to see where Petra grew up.

Her reaction, a simple smile and a kiss but I could tell it meant more to her than just that.

Monday March 7th

Oh dear.

Darth pulled me in to her office first thing this morning to tell me the news. At her meeting on Friday she was informed, along with her peers, that by the end of the day the changes would be announced. At three o'clock she was pulled aside by her current boss' boss to be told that she was being kept on, but would be replacing her boss. I have only met him a few times, but I think he made Darth do most of his work whilst taking the praise himself. It transpires that his cover has been blown and as such has been relieved of his duties.

What this means for me is that I have to take on more responsibility from Darth, whilst still managing the current team. I will get a promotion out of the changes, albeit, not much of a rise in salary. Darth is happy with the changes and I gather she was not too fond of her previous boss anyway.

The changes have to start straight away, so Darth will be in London for most of the week. I will also be expected to travel down to London now and again. I am still in shock at the speed this has happened. Nevertheless I still have a job, have been promoted and have received a small increase to my salary. I guess I have done quite well out of these cut backs.

If I am not careful, however, I may turn into Linda.

Tuesday March 8th

Crazy day at work today and I am well and truly into my new role. Three meetings were scheduled in my diary and this took up most of my time today. I have also been informed that I have to make my first trip to London on Friday (Darth will already be there). I spoke to the staff this morning to discuss the changes and to reiterate that their own jobs are safe. They seemed quite pleased for me; however, I suspect that they are happier about the news that they shall see less of Darth.

I stopped off for a coffee on the way home and told Petra my news. She was obviously delighted for me and came round the counter to give me a big hug, despite the queue of people waiting to be served. I sat at my usual table and noticed that Petra has made a little 'Reserved' sign which she must place on my table when she is working. When it had quietened down, she came over and joined me for a chat. She said that Linda had called last night and the shopping trip had been arranged for this Saturday. We agreed to meet up on Sunday again and head over to Dads.

When I got home, the phone was ringing and it was Mike. He wants to come over on Thursday night after work and take up on my offer for a chat. I agreed to prepare something in the way of food and I know that Mike is a fussy eater (not in a bad way, it just needs to be healthy, organic, prepared properly, etc,).

With the snooker already booked for tomorrow night, it is turning into a busy week.

Wednesday March 9th

After the madness of yesterday, today turned out to be really quiet at work. Darth is staying in London until Friday and e-mailed to say that she will be flying back with me (oh, the joy.). I had two meetings booked for today; however, they were both cancelled at the last minute. This gave me the opportunity to spend some time with Sue to see how she was getting on. I must admit, I was really impressed by how quickly she is picking things up and it doing incredibly well at the moment.

Wills was in great form tonight and we spent the whole night verbally abusing each other to a near art form. I will choose not to repeat too much of what was said to protect the reader, however, he did tear into me about not being able to find a suitable Scottish girlfriend. Of course, I replied that he was incapable of finding a suitable older girlfriend. He then said something about getting a job with the Immigration department to help with my courting whereas I suggested he get a job behind the bar at the Students Union. The snooker frames were lasting an age tonight, so when he tied the match at two frames all, we agreed to call it a night.

We were both in great form in the humour department, but the snooker was absolutely awful.

Thursday March 10th

Mike arrived at the flat at just before seven o'clock. I had finished work early and headed home to make dinner. In true Mike style, I prepared a healthy, organic meal which was also vegetarian (ensuring I ticked all the boxes); however, Mike arrived with eight bottles of beer so I guess he might not have been too bothered what I made.

By the time he had finished the first bottle, he was off on a verbal rant and I saw, for the first time, a very different side to him. He confirmed he had had enough now and was making his plans to leave. He and Lucy have been avoiding each other constantly and Mike has spent the last week sleeping in the spare room. He is only glad that Lewis is too young to know what is going on.

My second beer lay untouched on the coffee table as Mike polished off his sixth. At that point (being only an occasional drinker) he was in no state to go home so I suggested he spend the night here. I also suggested that I call Lucy to let her know as I did not want him to add fuel to the fire. When I called I could tell she was severely pissed off, but she stopped short of giving me a hard time over it. I think she could tell by my voice I was most uncomfortable about the whole situation. Despite my loyalty to Mike, I am also fond of Lucy and the whole affair is distressing to me also.

So it is off to bed for me, with a heavily snoring Mike on my sofa.

Friday March 11th

It is not long before midnight and Mike has just left. We spent the day at the flat talking everything over. Mike awoke with the most almighty of hangovers and I didn't sleep to well last night with the noise coming from the sofa. As such, I took a days annual leave and Mike did the same before going back to sleep. He did not stir again until just after one o'clock.

After a very late breakfast, which Mike barely touched, he confessed that he has not been sleeping well of late. This has made the situation with Lucy even worse as he said that he is irritable at the slightest thing. This is also having a knock on effect with his work and he said that he needs to get things sorted quickly.

I suggested that we meet up with the others tonight, but he just wanted to stay in and talk. I told him that he will need to tell the others sooner or later but for now he wants to deal with it his own way. I advised that he should talk to Linda, maybe get a female's perspective, but he was not for having that (I sensed at that point a bit of anger towards the suggestions, so I quickly changed the subject).

I thought for one moment he would never leave, however, after another cup of coffee he thanked me, hugged me and left for home.

'Off to face the music', he quipped as I closed the door behind him.

Somehow, I do not think there will be any dancing.

Saturday March 12th

Petra called me this morning and asked if I would look after Lukas today. Lucie is not 100% and she didn't want to let down Linda on their planned trip. I said I would be delighted to take him and agreed to meet them all at the train station.

I received hugs from them all and Lukas and I waved them off to their shopping haven of Glasgow. Lukas and I then took a trip to the toy department of Jenners before heading to the same at John Lewis. We (ok, I) choose a Star Wars Lego set and then I took him to Dynamic Earth.

We arrived back at the flat around four o'clock and, after Petra had called to confirm all was well, we spent an hour or so trying to build one of the space crafts. I've never been good at Lego but Lukas kept me right. After dinner, I put on a movie and he fell asleep on the sofa just as Petra and Linda arrived. I made some coffee and carried Lukas through to the spare room and couldn't help but smile as Petra and Linda relayed their stories from earlier with much laughter shared between them.

Linda has just left and Petra is having a shower before bed.

And, I just couldn't be happier at the moment.

Sunday March 13th

Just before nine o'clock, we all had breakfast which in my flat comprises of toast and Coco Pops. Lukas did not seem fazed at all about staying overnight at my flat, which was a bit of a relief as I was not sure how he may react this morning. Once we had cleared away the dishes, we headed over to Petra's flat to see how Lucie was feeling.

I must admit that I was quite shocked to see how pale she was, however, Petra and I did manage to convince her to make an appointment with the doctor tomorrow. She said she was feeling better, but wanted to stay in bed for the day.

We left her alone and headed over to Dads for the weekly feed. I rang the doorbell and was surprised to see Mary open the door. I gave her a hug and walked in, doing the same to Dad who had just came through from the kitchen (taking the opportunity to whisper a little teasing remark into his ear).

When we had all settled in, I had to go and 'see a man about a dog'. After successfully completing the task, I decided to have a walk into my old room. It is now the spare room but I can almost feel the history of it and often pop in for a moments thought and reflection. Now I have no idea what possessed me to do so, however, I had a notion to go into Dad's room (I think I must have been deep in memories at this point). When I got there, I noticed some make up and perfume on the dresser. After a quick 'Cross-Dressing Dad' vision, I noticed that the wardrobe door was open and some of Mary's clothes were hanging up (Dad would never fit into those – panic over.).

I decided to keep my findings to myself (for the moment) and headed back down stairs. The rest of the day was the usual Sunday dinner, piano, chat and chess (Dad has started to teach Lukas).

When we returned back to Petra's flat, and put Lukas to bed, I told Petra about my findings (leaving out the part about my initial concerns). She asked how I felt about it and I said that not only was I fine about it, but happy for him. Having reflected on it, I truly am delighted for them both. She gave me her usual hug, kiss and smile and as I walked home I could feel my eyes starting to well up.

Of course, it was the cold windy evening in Edinburgh that caused it.

Monday March 14th

Back to work, back to Darth, back to bedlam. Well, it was fine actually; I just decided to go a bit James Blunt there.

It was an early finish for me today, as I had my monthly meeting to attend to and wanted to get there early. It was really busy tonight and there were some new attendees. I am surprised at the age of some of them, as they seem so young (or is it that I am getting older?). I always fear and hope in equal measures for the new recruits. It is easy attending the first meeting, it is the coming back every month after that which is the real struggle.

I headed back to the flat with my mind racing. By the time I went indoors it was undertaking its own Formula One Grand Prix. I am worried about Lucie (Petra called to say the appointment was on Wednesday), therefore, worried about Petra and Lukas. I am worried about Mike, therefore, worried about Lucy. I am worried about Linda and the amount of work she is doing. To a lesser extent, I am also worried about Wills and Alex and their personal struggles with relationships and art. On top of all this, I have received three threatening notes that suggest that someone wants to kill me.

I made a coffee (the one addiction I can never give up) and headed to my desk. There is a small drawer hidden in the centre of the desk that locks. I took out my key, opening the drawer and removing the sole contents which are the three notes. I read them one by one and tossed the words over in my head. Hoax or real? Hoax or real?

I picked up the phone and rang Alex; it was time to share this with my most trusted of allies. He has agreed to come over tomorrow for dinner, but he has insisted on cooking himself. A small price to pay for what I will be confiding in him when he arrives.

Although, I'm not sure what I am most nervous about, his cooking or revealing my darkest of secrets.

Tuesday March 15th

Work = Meetings = More Meetings = Boredom = I left at 5 o'clock.

Alex appeared at six o'clock just after I had changed. He had a Waitrose bag (he would not dream of shopping elsewhere) that was ready to burst with the weight of his ingredients. He acknowledged me with a wink and a nod before heading to the kitchen. 'Let the magic begin' he screamed from the kitchen in his best Brian Blessed voice. I swear he is like a 35 year old version, minus the beard (at the moment). Indecently, Alex arrived wearing a three piece suit; however, being him it was of a deep purple velvet variety.

I left him thrashing about in my kitchen with equal measures of vocabulary genius and cursing being shouted out through the doorway until he arrived with the finished article. Now, I have no idea what was placed in front of me (and Alex is not one to divulge his culinary secrets to anyone), suffice it to say, it was absolutely delicious. 'Just something I picked up in my travels' is his standard response.

I packed the plates in the dishwasher and took the red wine through to the sitting room where Alex had made himself comfortable on the sofa. I handed him his glass and walked over the desk and took my seat. I unlocked the drawer and pulled out the three notes before handing them to Alex and watching closely his reaction. To my surprise he burst out laughing, however, when he lifted his head from reading the last note his expression changed.

'Surely some manner of poor hoax, Old Boy' he suggested.

I confirmed that there had been no takers and no clues as to the author. Alex confessed that it was neither his doing nor was he aware of any culprit. He thought it had Wills 'name written all over it or maybe Mike at an off chance, however, it was certainly not the style that Alex himself would adopt. I agreed as much, hence, the reason I had approached him. I did not go in to any more detail at this stage; I guess I just needed another point of view. I value Alex's opinion greatly and if he thinks there is nothing in it then who I am to disagree?

'I would suggest that this may be the end of the matter and the hoaxer, of incredulous poor taste, will bring themselves forward.'

And I hope he is right.

Wednesday March 16th

Although I am not so sure he is.

It happened on the way home from work tonight. I took my usual route home and although it was dark, I swear I saw someone emerge from the shadows. I'm sure it was a male, but it was too dark to see properly as the street lighting was not working at that stretch of the road. Now, maybe paranoia is starting to set in, but I thought the figure was following me, I have no proof of this as I was too spooked to look around. I just don't know for sure, it was just a feeling I had.

When I reached the (relative) safety of my flat, I closed the curtains and turned on a table lamp in my bedroom. I then returned to the darkness of the sitting room and looked out from the window to the street below. To my relief, or disappointment (I'm not sure which), there was nothing suspicious on the street below. It was filled with fellow late commuters, a few groups of students and a drunken figure trying to sell a Metro newspaper.

I decided to shower and make some dinner, settling for a large coffee to follow. After I had settled, I called Petra to find out about Lucie. She said she was looking better and the doctor had taken some blood samples. I just hope it is not serious.

For Lucie or me.

Thursday March 17th

Darth called me into her office today. She said that she was due in London tomorrow, but had to take the day off. As I missed the last meeting, she suggested that I take her place. I told her that I would be delighted to take her place (no Mike to ruin this week's plans I hope.) and she suggested that it would 'make a good impression'.

I decided to make arrangements to fly down tonight and book into a hotel. I checked on the staff before I left and they are currently operating like a well oiled machine (if I say so myself). I booked a flight for 8:15 tonight which will get me to London a little over an hour later.

When I got home, I skipped dinner and called Petra. No word from the doctors yet, however, Lucie is in good spirits by all account. When I hung up the phone, Alex called me shortly afterwards. I told him about my potential follower and of a previous late night visitor. I also explained that the notes have been arriving on the first day of each month. He suggested that the follower was most likely a result of my paranoia, however, if a further note comes in April I should call the police.

I hung up the phone and packed an overnight bag for London. The taxi is picking me up in about twenty minutes.

I think a night away from here might just do me some good.

Friday March 18th

The hotel was basic, despite the astronomical London rate, however, by the time I arrived it was a place to eat and sleep. The meeting went well and it was very interesting to see things from a different perspective. It was obvious that Darth is well respected by her peers and that her previous boss was not.

The flight back up to Edinburgh was smooth (thankfully) and I got home at around nine o'clock. I was too worn out to think about going out so I played a little blues on the guitar and decided to write today's entry before setting down for an early night.

And see what the weekend will bring.

Saturday March 19th

Oh why did I agree to this?

Wills called me this morning and asked if I would go on a 'double date' with Petra and Kylie. I attentively agreed and called Petra with the news. To her eternal credit she has agreed to come, however, wants to get Lukas to bed before we go. Although Lucie seems to be better, she does not wish to burden her too much as she has been looking after him when Petra has been working her shifts in the coffee shop. Lucie has been told to call the doctor on Monday when the test results are due back.

Petra, Lukas and I spent the day all together. The weather was pretty awful so, after a failed attempt to visit the Museum of Childhood on the Royal Mile, we headed back to mine. I'm not one for video games, however, Wills bought me a console last year (I think to give him something to do when he visits). I don't have many games but I bought the Star Wars Lego game recently and that kept Lukas amused for a while.

Petra has just taken Lukas home and I am just about to have a shower and change before we go. May the force be with us.

Sunday March 20th

And it was truly awful.

I think Petra is still talking to me, however, she didn't say much to Kylie (I'm not convinced that she could understand most of what Kylie said). And to be fair also, Kylie did not give Petra much of an opportunity to speak anyway. Fortunately, we got some respite when the movie started, albeit, it was the latest Hollywood blockbuster and was simply terrible (albeit, less terrible than listening to Kylie for a further 2 hours).

We headed for drinks afterwards with Petra and I calling it a night when Kylie suggested a trip to her favourite nightclub. Wills departed with her and I am sure that I sensed an almost apologetic look in his eyes.

Today, we headed over to Dads early and it was Dad who answered the door. He announced that Mary was cooking dinner today and I am sure he could read my teasing smile like a book. The dinner was delicious and I can tell that she cooks well (which should keep Dad more than happy.). This friendship with Dad is only weeks old (for all I know) but already I see a little weight being put on my fathers midriff.

I walked Petra and Lukas back to their flat and promised to call Petra tomorrow to find out how Lucie got on.

Monday March 21st

Lucie has been taken into hospital for further tests and Petra is beside herself with worry. Having been through an awful time with the illness, then death, of my own mother I can understand how she feels. Of course, I am not best suited to give advice on the subject given my decline into drug abuse after her death. I have never blamed her death for my addiction, only myself and the wrong choices I made at the time.

I agreed to go to the hospital tomorrow night with Petra as Lukas will be staying with a friend from school (who is also Czech) to allow us to go up alone. I will do my best to support Petra, but I must admit I am not good in hospitals.

And I am dreading it already...

Tuesday March 22nd

We are just back from the hospital and fortunately it was good news. The initial tests were showing a low blood count, however, it has improved already and the doctor thinks she will be out by the end of the week. I could see that she was looking visibly better when we arrived and that had an immediate effect on Petra.

As we were heading home, Petra started to question whether her caring for Lukas was having an impact. Petra stated that she has been working more and more shifts and leaving Lukas with Lucie. I tried to reassure her but I can tell it is troubling her.

I just hope that I can be of some support, however small.

Wednesday March 23rd

If I adjust my eyes I can see my clock says 11:38 pm. Woo Hoo, I HAVE MADE IT!!!!!!!!!!!!! DEADLINE BEATEN!!!!!!!!!!

Snooker with Wills, the Willstar, Jack E Boy was great and I pumped him HA HA HA. 4 -1 to Steveo – WHOOOOO'S THE DADDY!!!!

Wills and I drunk and drank and drunk stuff, although I'm no, not too sure what that green stuff was we were downing at the end. It was tasty though, yes indeedy doo daaa.

I have taken tomorrow off, as I thought tonight, hair down time and I was letting go.

AND I THINK I WENT!!!!!!!!!!!!!!!!!!!!!!!!!!!

Thursday March 24th

Oh Lord, my head still feels like it has been exposed to some type of volcanic activity. I must admit, I do not remember writing much of yesterday's entry (or any reference to a green drink).

I stayed in bed until the afternoon and spent most of the time on the sofa. I tried to read a book, however, was struggling to focus on the page. When I eventually did, I realised that it was in Czech (I never realised I picked up the book Petra gave me). I fancied some light relief so I put on a few stand up comic DVD's but I ended up falling asleep through most of them.

I had a light dinner (being unsure if I would be able to retain it in my stomach) and gave the flat a clean. I picked up the guitar afterwards; however, my head made my hand put it back.

So now it is early to bed for me as it is back to work tomorrow.

Friday March 25th

Darth is back down in London; however, she felt the need to call me at half past seven this morning. My presence was requested for a meeting next week but Darth talked them out of it (bless her - I am really not up for another flight).

I feel now is time for a bit of a confession. I do not like to fly. In fact, I hate it. Actually, I should say that I am petrified of flying. It may be the safest form of travel but when it goes tits up, it really goes tits up. The company are still intent in flying staff between Edinburgh and London; however, I prefer getting the train. Unfortunately, Darth loves to fly and hates trains so I am fighting a losing battle.

Maybe I should go more eco-friendly in the office and start dropping some hints.

Saturday March 26th

I pulled out of a planned get together with the other guys tonight as Lucie is getting out of hospital. The three of us went to meet her and I arranged for a taxi back to the flat. Although not back to her usual self, Lucie certainly looks much better.

When we got back to the flat, we made a bed up for Lucie in the sitting room. I think she was keen to watch some decent television after her hospital visit. Petra and I got Lukas to bed and then she asked me to stay over. Having agreed, I have nipped home for some fresh clothes and pyjamas (got to keep myself decent) and to write today's entry.

And from this day forward, this diary is travelling with me everywhere.

Sunday March 27th

All is good and well with the world and I am writing this after another wonderful night with Petra. I told her about my little bet with Alex and she was very encouraging. She even suggested that I try to write a book, but one thing at a time. I was a little nervous about telling her in case she wanted to read it; however, she appreciates that it is personal and should remain so.

Lucie is looking much better and she confessed that she had had the best night's sleep for a long time. I suggested that she come to Dads with us, but she declined suggesting maybe another day. Petra requested that she pass also, as she wanted to spend time with Lucie which is understandable.

I headed over to Dads and gave him a big bear hug when he answered the door. Mary was in the sitting room watching a quiz show, so I offered to help Dad in the kitchen after saying hello. I could not help myself but to tease him and stated something about her spending so much time here, she should move in. He then confessed that she had and he looked worried, however, I told him I knew and that I was happy for them both. This, of course, led to further teasing and as usual Dad took it in good spirits. I do, however, sense that he is hiding something further but time will tell I'm sure.

We had a nice meal and a few games of chess before I retired early. Mary gave me a hug and kiss goodnight which was nice as I guess it must be difficult for her too.

Monday March 28th

Back to work today and it was another early meeting with Darth. One of the other managers is off work with stress and she asked if I could cover his team in the meantime. I of course agreed, however, I had difficulty hiding my shock at the news. Although I am not too close in terms of friendship to him, I know him well enough through working with him since I started. He is married with two sons, so I hope that everything turns out alright for him.

I held a meeting with his team to explain the situation as best I could. I was tied up in HR red tape when it came to answering their questions, but for once (and for his sake) I was quite happy to avoid such questions. My own team are doing well and are meeting all their workload targets. The team seem to gel well together and there have been no issues since the sacking of Sam. I feel fortunate that I can just leave them to get on with their work (of course, it's all down to my excellent management skills.)

When I got home, I called Linda at her house to see how she was doing. With my colleague off with stress, it just heightened my concern for my friend. When she answered she was quite curt with me and said that she was too busy to talk. I told her about my colleague and my concern for her and she said I was not to worry about her; she was fine and not working as hard. She hung up the phone before I could find out what she meant. I then called Wills to arrange snooker for Wednesday. That was a more enjoyable call and he is looking forward to it. He has promised that we will not be drinking as much as last week as even he suffered (he forgot about the green drink as well.). I finally called Mike to see how he was doing, however, Lucy answered and said he was out and before I asked she shouted
'No, I do not know where he is'

It was nearly ten o'clock when I called and not like him to be out this late during the week (except, of course, the time he turned up at my flat). I tried his mobile but it was switched off.

I just hope he is alright.

Tuesday March 29th

I got a text from Mike this morning saying he was fine and he just went out after work. He has promised to meet up soon and asked me not to worry. I just wish it was that easy.

At work, I have realised that the advantage of me looking after an extra team is that I do not have to go to London (and therefore avoid flying). Darth confirmed she will cover any meetings that I may have had to attend for the time being. The 'Other' team (as I will refer to them) are testing the water of having a temporary new boss. I will keep a close eye on them, however, I am savvy enough to spot the potential 'trouble makers' (two), the 'manage closely' (two) and the 'leave them to get on with it' (one). My own team continue to cause little concern.

Alex called this evening to see how I was. He is no closer than I to finding a guilty party to the hoax/threat. He is coming over on Sunday and will be coming to Dads. Alex is very fond of Dad and keen to meet his 'Special Friend' (as he refers to Mary). Petra is working on Sunday so we will do something on Saturday together.

Wednesday March 30th

I have decided to take Friday off from work. It is not ideal with having to manage the new team, however, Darth said it would be fine as she is in Edinburgh and would look after things. I did not sleep much last night thinking about the notes and, with this Friday being the first of the month; I thought I would prepare myself. Deep down, I guess I still think this will turn out to be a hoax, so I plan to stay up and catch them in the act. At present though, I shall keep this to myself.

I held a meeting with the other team and set some ground rules. I offered my 'open door' policy should anyone have any issues they wish to discuss, but I think they will be fine. I spent some time with my own team today and sat beside each one in turn this afternoon. Everything is well up to date, their work is very accurate and there are no pressing issues that need to be dealt with. Sue said that she was enjoying the role and is getting through her share of the work quicker and with better accuracy to the rest of the team. I just wish a few more were like her.

Wills and I had a good time at snooker, settling on a 2-2 draw (for those interested). He said things are starting to cool a little with Kylie as she is spending more time with her friends and he prefers it when they are alone. He knows what other people must think of her, but claims she is very different when it is just the two of them together. I can see that he is once again concerned how things are between them, but it is for him to sort out.

I have enough to worry about.

Thursday March 31st

I headed over to see Petra tonight after work as she was finishing her shift. She looked down and was very quiet as I drank my coffee at my table. When she closed up the shop, she suggested that we go for a walk before she went home.

We headed up towards Bruntsfield Links in near silence, making just small talk about the weather and the new café that had just opened up round the corner. As we walked, hand in hand, across the old golf course she hit me with her news. Lucie has decided to go back to the Czech Republic. After her recent hospital visit, and although it turned out that everything was fine, she realised that she wanted to head home. I was a little shocked, but could understand her reasons. The next piece of news I was not expecting as much.

Petra could be going with her.

I must admit I was speechless. All right, we have only been dating for a couple of months but I can tell we have something special. I wanted to ask a hundred different questions but settled on one.

'What about us?'

Petra's eyes filled, but she did not have an answer. She couldn't see how she could stay in Edinburgh without the support of Lucie and I can see that. Will a long distance relationship work, or will it be like a teenage holiday romance? Is it maybe just better to end it before it goes any further?

I walked Petra back to her flat in a deeper silence than we left the coffee shop. When we reached the door I held her for what felt like an eternity. Full blown tears had arrived at this point and it took both of us a while to compose ourselves. I suggested that we meet Saturday, as planned, to talk things over – just the two of us and she agreed.

At that, she retreated and I headed home with more than the Edinburgh breeze watering my eyes.

Friday April 1st

No note today.

After spending the night battling to keep myself awake on the sofa, the perpetrator did not show after all. I called Alex to talk things over and he arrived at the flat thirty minutes later. The sight of a three piece pinstripe suit with matching 1940's Trilby hat at least put a smile on my face. He tried to reassure me that it must have been a hoax all along and that the sightings and late night visits were just my imagination running away with me. Alex thought my immediate concern should be the potential loss of Petra.

He said that I had changed greatly, and for the better, since Petra and I have been together and that I should do what I could to save the relationship. I suggested that it had only been a couple of months but he had his reply ready.

'Stephen my dear, dear friend, you realise that you are not getting any younger. Petra is a wonderful girl, a shining beacon of light in the darkness of your soul. She is someone who most certainly is worth the fight and resolve to remain in your life. I pray you consider the potential consequences of letting her go. You may end up miserable, alone, or even worse. You may end up like our good friend Jack and I for one could and would not tolerate another Kylie, Old Boy.'

And with a smile and a laugh, he had said it all.

Saturday April 2nd

I spent the morning cleaning the flat and getting everything organised for Petra's visit. Lukas is having a sleep over with his friend and Lucie is spending the day resting. Petra, I understand, spent the morning cleaning her flat also so that Lucie would indeed rest. She arrived for lunch and I had prepared something light for us to eat. We sat, mostly in silence, and Petra played with her food rather than eating it.

I told her that I cared for her greatly and that I didn't want her to go back. I understood her reasons, but selfishly, I wanted her to stay. She said she felt the same way and wanted to stay, however, she knew that she would return to the Czech Republic at some point. I did see a glimmer of hope though, when she looked straight at me and said.

'I have not decided for sure, yet.'

It was all I needed to hear. I leapt to my feet and kneeled beside her, taking her hand. I told her that we should stop worrying about what may not happen. That we should just enjoy ourselves and see what happens. We enjoyed each others company so much, that we should just continue and see what life throws at us. If she decides to go home, then we deal with that. If she decides to stay, then we continue as we are. I have lived my life without regret and do not want to look back thinking 'what if?' and Petra just smiled and nodded in agreement.

We retreated to the sofa and put on a movie but, in all honesty, we didn't see much of it. She declined the offer to stay over as she wanted to go back and check on Lucie and spend some time with her. She did, however, agree to stay for dinner.

And we 'hit' the sofa again before she left.

Sunday April 3rd

It came last night.

I admit it, I took my eye off the ball thinking that it was just a hoax after all and Alex was right. He was not though, and the note arrived during the night whilst I was sleeping. When I discovered it, I decided against touching it and went to the kitchen where I found some tongs. I then found an A4 plastic wallet that I could place this one in, thinking I should try and preserve any potential evidence. I carefully unfolded it with the tongs, to allow me to read the contents, and placed it in the plastic wallet.

'Were you expecting this on the first Stephen? Well April Fool to you - it is time to expect the unexpected and believe me this is no fool.'

Now I am thankful that Petra did not stay over, for when I awoke this morning to find the note behind my front door, I struggled to maintain my emotions. I have decided now is the time to contact the police, however, I will wait until tomorrow.

Alex arrived at lunchtime dressed in tartan trousers, Aran sweater and Tam o' Shanter hat. Normally this would at least raise a smile from me, however, my expression must have allowed Alex to know instantly what was wrong and he asked to see the latest. He agreed that now was the time to contact the police. Our hoaxes never last this long, are never as serious as this and one or two of the others usually join in.

I had further discussions with Alex regarding Petra and he suggested that I was doing the right thing, however, to be careful that the notes did not affect the relationship. I told him that I fully intended to keep them both separate. He told me that I was to –

'Throw caution to the wind, in fact embrace it and ride it like a magical carpet through the desert'

Yes, he lost me too.

We headed over to Dads and he was delighted to see Alex again. Alex in turn made great fuss over Dad and Mary (in his usual, lovable, style). We had dinner, of which Alex insisted on helping Mary prepare, before retiring to the sitting room for coffee and chess. Alex refuses to play chess ('I am far too intellectually advanced for you both and I refuse to show you up in front of a lady') as Dad and I played a few games together. I lost all the games comfortably; however, I put this down to two reasons. Firstly, Alex kept putting me off with his

'Oh, what did you do that for Steve?' and

'Not the move an intelligent player would have made, Old Boy.' comments.

Secondly, I kept thinking about the note, and what I am going to say to the police tomorrow.

Monday April 4th

I went into work this morning but decided to take a half day. I wanted to get my head (and story) straight before speaking to the police. I spent the early part of the afternoon going over what had happened and, more importantly, why. That latter question I still have no answer to.

The phone call was not a pleasant experience and, pretty much, a waste of time. After holding on the phone for an age, I was put through to Detective Sergeant Jeff Stone. DS Stone is obviously from the 'Bad Cop' side of the operation. After giving him the full story, he asked whether it could be some type of practical joke and did my group of friends undertake of such activities. I stated that I thought it had gone past that stage but he said that he sees hundreds of these types of threats that turn out to be nothing more than a prank and waste of police time.

I came off the call both deflated and angry. I paced around the flat mentally seeking answers. I need to get to the bottom of this one way or another, even if I have to investigate it myself.

At that point, I remembered a party that I had attended a number of years ago. An old school friend had also been in attendance and we had chatted for a while about our school years together. It turns out that he had just joined the forensic science department of Strathclyde Police in Glasgow. We had been good friends at school but lost contact when we headed to university as he headed south to an English University.

Desperate times call for desperate measures, so I registered myself on Facebook. With a name like Lars Tebsin he was not difficult to find and I was delighted that he was a fully committed member. I sent him a request to be his 'friend' (man, this is like being back at school again) and await his reply.

I just hope he will be able to help.

Tuesday April 5th

It is like waiting for a kettle to boil.

I went into work today, but kept checking my phone for an update from Lars. I'm now worried he won't reply even though we got on so well at school and when we met at the party it was like we hadn't been apart.

I left work early and called Petra from home. She is fine and both Lucie and Lukas are doing well. I must admit that I was a little distracted when I was speaking to her as I kept hitting the refresh button on the computer awaiting a Facebook update. After I hung up, Wills called to firm up our snooker plans for tomorrow. He has news for me but wants to wait until tomorrow to give me the full story.

It is now nearing a quarter to midnight and I have just undertaken my final refresh to no success – so it is off to bed for me.

Wednesday April 6th

Three big pieces of news today and I don't know where to start. Let go chronologically.

My colleague Iain, who was off with stress, has resigned so I will need to look after the other team until a replacement is sought. Darth told me today and I sense that there is more to this story but not for me to know just yet I guess (Darth, I am sure, will tell me in her own time).

Wills has split up with Kylie. I guess it was on the cards but I know that he was fond of her despite her faults (and his faults too.). I believe that it was an amicable split although he did not want to go into much detail. He said that he realised that it was time to get on with his life and he was in the process of a serious change in career. Again, he was keeping details to himself (he is turning into Alex I swear.); however, for this I am very intrigued (he was also only drinking cokes tonight). Wills has not had a 'proper' job since he left university having had so many temporary jobs that I have lost count (as has he.).

Finally, Lars added me as a friend with a message about it taking me long enough to get into the twenty first century. I found out having logged on when I returned home from the snooker and I immediately sent him a message requesting that we meet up some day that it suited.

So part one of the great investigation is complete.

Thursday April 7th

I met with Petra after work this evening. She was finishing off her shift when I arrived and seemed in good spirits. When I told her about Wills separating with Kylie, this cheered her up (and I was thankful for the topic of conversation). She said that she had found it incredibly difficult to talk to Kylie as they had nothing in common. She also confessed to getting a headache after every time they met. I told her that I suffered just the same.

We went for a short walk before heading back to Petra's flat. We talked and joked and had a nice time. I think we both must have thought it best not to discuss anything too serious tonight. I popped in to say hello to Lucie before heading home. During my time with Petra, I had forgotten all about Facebook and the notes, however, it hit me when I reached my front door. I rushed over to the computer and logged straight onto Facebook, ignoring a few requests from people I went to school with to become 'friends' (I didn't like most of them when I was at school – what has changed now?). Lars had confirmed he would be in Edinburgh for a concert on Saturday and could meet for a quick drink beforehand. He also said that he was free next Saturday if I fancied a trip through to Glasgow to see him. I quickly replied to him that I would meet him in a pub on Rose Street at four o'clock on Saturday and we could chat then.

Friday April 8th

Work was pretty uneventful, with a call from Darth the highlight of my working day. She took some time out of her meeting in London to say that some of the senior staff members were asking after me and they wanted her to pass on their thanks for stepping in to help. Darth commented that I must have made a good first impression on them – and that I was not to let her down.

Petra and I met at the Filmhouse Café after work and were joined by Alex and Linda. We all discussed Wills' situation and the pending big career move. We had a few guesses of what that might entail – recruitment consultant, stockbroker, underwear/sunglasses model, the adult entertainment business? I went to the bar to buy a round of drinks and Linda appeared by my side. She wanted to apologise for the being sharp with me the other night. She said that I had caught her at a really bad time and appreciates that I care for her. She said that she has been working more sensible hours and now goes out at lunch time for a walk and admitted that getting out of the office for an hour was making her feel much better.

When we returned with the drinks Alex was taking a phone call (lots of 'darlings' were heard). When he hung up, he dismissed the drinks I had just bought and shouted over to the waitress to bring over Champagne. His short film script has been sold and filming is to start next week. I am truly delighted for him.

Not that his ego needs any further inflating.

Saturday April 9th

It was great to see Lars again and he has hardly changed in all these years.

We met up as planned and he was there with John, one of his colleagues from work. I felt a little sorry for John as we spent so much time talking about our school days that he must have felt left out a bit. Lars and I laughed so much that it hurt and had John not been there, they would have missed the concert as we both lost track of time. We swapped phone numbers and agreed to speak again during the week and finalise plans to meet up next Saturday in Glasgow.

I walked home from Rose Street back to flat in good spirits and then realised that I had momentarily forgotten the reason for meeting with Lars. Obviously, with John there I would not have brought up the subject of the notes, however, I was surprised how is slipped my mind again. It seems that when I am in company I forget all about these threats but, when I am alone, it all comes back.

I do, however, plan that my meeting with Lars next week will be very different.

Sunday April 10th

Dad called to cancel dinner today as Mary is feeling a little poorly. I asked him to pass on my best wishes and agreed to see him next week as normal.

Petra and the others are away on a family trip today over to Fife. They plan to spend the day in St Andrews as Lucie is very fond of watching golf whenever it is shown on television (she has never played though). As such, she is desperate to see the Old Course before she goes home.

All this left me with a day to myself so I started by giving the flat a thorough clean before doing the same to the guitar. I decided to sort out the bookcase and rearrange the furniture a bit too. I called Alex to update him on my plan and the meeting with Lars. He suggested that it was a good idea (in principle), however, I should proceed with caution.

So proceed with caution, I shall.

<u>Monday April 11th</u>

When I was kid, my friends and I used to play a game called 'Chappie'. It basically consisted of someone chapping the door of a stranger's house and running away before the home owner answered.

Now this, on the face of it, was always seen as a bit of harmless fun by my group of friends. Last night, however, it turned out to be a bit of a nightmare for me. The first 'chap' came around half past one this morning. I was in the middle of a deep sleep and it took me a while to get my bearings. When I realised what was happening, I rushed to the door; however, by the time I got there no one was standing before me. This, as you can imagine, unsettled, me greatly. I returned to my bed, however, spent the next two hours tossing and turning before finally drifting off to sleep once more. The next 'chap' came at just after a half past four. I woke from my restless sleep and ran once more to the door; however, once again no one was before me. I looked down the stairs and saw no one and heard nothing, not even the main door to the flats closing.

So that was me awake until it was time to get ready for work. By lunch time I was absolutely exhausted and I finally left work around four o'clock. I made myself a light dinner before lying down on the sofa to watch the six o'clock news. I did not see much past the main headlines before being awakened by the start of the ten o'clock news.

I just hope that this was a one off, as I do not cope well without my sleep.

Tuesday April 12th

I slept a bit better last night, albeit, I was still a little restless. At one point I thought I heard footsteps outside my front door, although, it may have just been my imagination and I never left my bed to find out. When I did wake this morning my mind was racing once again about the knocking on the door. I could not get my head around how there was no sight or sound of the person. I then had a thought and, putting down my cereal, I headed to my front door. There is situated, just outside my door, a small cupboard that contains some cleaning items. It is used by the cleaner of all the apartment stairwells throughout the development. I had a look at the door and there were some marking around the lock as if it had been forced open. The door was once again locked; however, I suspect that it may have been used as a temporary hid out. I decided to mentally place this information on the backburner as I had to get myself ready for work. When I arrived, Darth pulled me in for a meeting. She ran through the latest update from her last London meeting. For my point, all is well and Darth is pushing things forward as she tends to do. Then she gave me the news I had been expecting, if not the content.

Iain (my now ex-colleague) has resigned as he had, correctly, guessed that he was going to be sacked. It turns out that Iain has been having an affair with Sam and was party to the selling of client information. It transpires that he had built up quite a substantial gambling debt and had used his relationship with Sam to repay this. As for now, his marriage is now over (as you would expect) and he is living with Sam.

I'm not sure how Darth got all this information from him, but she has her methods.

I must admit though, I certainly did not see that one coming.

Wednesday April 13th

I had my meeting last night. It was a busy night once again and most of the new attendees from last month were there again, so that was really positive. It has been so long since I used drugs that I am one hundred per cent positive that I will never again, however, these meetings bring that message home every time I attend.

After work, this evening, I met Wills for our weekly snooker match. He is handling life without Kylie well and, yes, he is still currently unattached. I asked him more about his big career move and he confirmed that he has a final interview on Friday. Again, he would not divulge any further information at this time, so I will just have to be patient.

But another evening off the beer was again intriguing.

Thursday April 14th

Darth has started the recruitment process to find a replacement for Iain. She has already asked me to assist with the selection and interview process (although I suspect that she will be making all the selections and I will be agreeing with her.).

After work I went to see Petra at the coffee shop. She seemed happy and pleased to see me. Again we avoided the 'Czech

Subject' (as I now refer to the matter). I know that we will have to discuss it again though I just want to enjoy my time with her at the moment.

We went for our usual walk after she closed up. It was a pleasant evening weather wise (for Edinburgh in April at least) and the walk was enjoyable. The only downside was that I found myself a little on edge tonight. I kept looking over my shoulder and watching doorways and alleys for someone watching or following us. At one point, Petra asked if I was ok. I quickly pulled myself together and assured her that I was fine.

Although, I think this shows that this whole affair is getting to me more than I originally thought.

Friday April 15th

Petra is out tonight with a friend, so I decided to have a night of phone calls to catch up with everyone. I started with Wills; however, I could not get hold of him to ask how his interview went. I guess I will find out soon enough.

I then called Alex who, as expected, was still in fine spirits.

'Simply marvellous, Old Boy. Totting off to see some filming of my own personal little ditty next week. It is surely the upstart of a magical beginning into the world of the motion picture art form.'

Linda was also having a quiet night in and was happy to have a catch up chat. I discussed the 'Czech Subject' with her and she was sorry to hear about it. She said that she had thoroughly enjoyed her day with Petra and planned to arrange another outing with her. Linda also said that she is still doing well, keeping up with her lunch time walks and sensible hours.

I then called Mike and, for once, reached him at home (albeit, Lucy was out for the evening). I asked how things were going and he confirmed that they were at least talking now and being civil to each other. He is still unsure whether his marriage will survive, but things have certainly improved.

Lars was last, and definitely not least, on my call list and we finalised arrangements for my trip to Glasgow tomorrow. We are meeting at Queen Street train station at twelve noon and we will take it from there.

And then, it all begins…

Saturday April 16th

I am writing this on the train back to Edinburgh. I have just had a great day with Lars which was perfectly concluded with his offer to help me with my situation.

We met as planned at the train station before heading to his favourite pub for some lunch. The place was playing rock music in the background, so it suited Lars perfectly being an avid fan of the loud stuff. We talked again about the old days and some of the things we got up to as kids, before talking about our lives since school. Lars has had an on/off relationship with a girl that we both went to school with (currently off.). He was always interested in science (which he always scored straight A's at school I seem to recall) and had an interest in forensics from an early age (influenced partly by the television programme Crimewatch - long before CSI started a wave of applications within this vocation in recent years.

I gave him an update on my life before finishing on my current situation with the notes. I explained this was part of the reason for getting in touch, but I would fully understand if he could not (or would not) get involved. He stated that, on the contrary, he would love to help and he was happy I got in touch regardless of the reason. He confirmed that he knew Sgt Stone but mostly through his senior officer, an Inspector Ed McCreedy, who was a personal friend. They met at training college and became close and Ed had always said he would make Inspector before he turned forty. Although he is only a few years older than us, he made the rank sooner than expected (apparently it also ruffled a few feathers within his peer group). He is said to be an excellent officer, who has followed up his promotion with some excellent results. He is very methodical, does things by the book and never gives up until he gets a result. Sgt Stone is a more old school type of officer who also gets results, however, has a reputation of using questionable methods (albeit nothing has been proven to this effect).

Lars said that he had a few days holiday coming up and he would come through to Edinburgh to see the notes for himself (he had previously told me to leave them in the flat and to avoid any further physical contact with them). Although not strictly by the book, he would bring some of his own equipment and see what he could find. He was also impressed that I took care of the last note before joking that I had watched too much CSI.

Truth be told though – I have never seen a single episode in my life.

Sunday April 17th

I feel, now that Lars is on board, that I might just get somewhere with this affair. I know that the police may get hundreds of pranks but I feel that I took due care and diligence not to go rushing to them until I was sure that there was more to this than just some sort of practical joke.

With my head feeling clearer than it has been for quite a while, I headed over to Dads. Petra, Lucie and Lukas are eating at friends today so I arrived alone. Mary is feeling much better, much to Dad's relief I could tell. She suspects that it was a mild form of food poisoning, albeit, she said it did not feel that mild at the time. I made some remark about Dad's cooking; however, Mary defended him wholeheartedly.

Chess was a closer affair this evening, with yours truly winning the deciding match. Even Mary was hooked as father and son battled it out for family pride. I sat with them for a while afterwards before making to leave. Dad saw me to the front door, but stopped me as I left.

'She's nice, Mary. Isn't she?' he asked.

I replied 'of course' and he just smiled at me. The answer, I suspect, he was looking for.

Monday April 18th

I spoke to Wills after work tonight and he confirmed that the interview went well. He expects to find out this week and agreed to tell me everything when we meet up for snooker on Wednesday night.

Lars called later on to firm up our plans for Saturday. We will meet up at twelve noon at Waverley train station and he confirmed that his agreement to help me is now on the proviso that I take him to the Hard Rock Café on George Street for lunch. A small price to pay I think.

Not long after Lars and I finished talking, the phone went again and this time it was Petra. She wants to come over tomorrow night as there are a few things that she feels we need to talk about. I expected that this was coming and I fully admit to sticking my head in the sand these last few weeks.

I guess it will now be time to face the truth and deal with matters.

Tuesday April 19th

Petra has just left and it turned out better than I had expected.

The family are all going to the Czech Republic to finalise arrangements for Lucie to move back home. They all leave on Saturday and will be gone for three weeks. Petra said that she wants to be there to help Lucie move back and settle in; however, Petra and Lukas are coming back after the three weeks. Her friends in Edinburgh have offered to help look after Lukas when required and Petra wants to see how that will work. I understand that Petra will return the favour when she can also.

I missed her terribly when she was away the last time and that was less than a week, although, I do think that the timing will be good as I need to focus on these notes and the help that Lars is going to give me. I realise that I may have the answer to this particular puzzle and Lars may just help me get there. So, with Petra and Lukas safely in the Czech Republic, I can really focus on getting to the bottom of this.

I just hope that three weeks is long enough.

Wednesday April 20th

Oh My Word. My good friend Wills has dumbfounded me once again.

I met him outside the snooker hall as usual, albeit, I did not recognise him at first. The trademark sunglasses were not on his head and no where to be seen. Also, his prized flowing locks have been cropped from his head. Now, Wills' hair was not very long, long and he certainly would not have won any air guitar or head-banging competitions with it. The hair style could best be described as 'Surfer Dude' long. Before me, however, stood Wills with a short back and sides haircut.

He kept me in suspense a little longer as we headed to the bar. I offered to buy the first round in celebration – a pint of good ale, a Jack Daniels or even Champagne (if they sold it in a snooker hall.). No, our Wills just wanted a fresh orange and soda water. So, at this point I was bursting. I grabbed him playfully and gave him a shake asking who he was and what he had done with my friend Wills. At this point, I noticed he had lost a little weight, not much (Wills has always been in good shape) and his biceps appeared a little bigger. He had the feel and appearance of the old rugby playing Wills that I recall from our university days. I let him go and demanded an answer.

And I got it.

Wills has been accepted into the fast track graduate program of the Lothian and Borders Police force.

Thursday April 21st

I may be wrong; it could have been a little more paranoia kicking in, though I think someone came after me tonight.

I finished work around six o'clock and headed straight home. I made a light dinner then changed into my running gear. I must admit to being a little inspired/jealous (delete as applicable.) of how Wills was looking last night.

I headed up to the Meadows and ran a couple of circuits before heading over the Bruntsfield Links. When I reached the other side, I headed down towards Tollcross and onto Lothian Road. I then decided to turn up one of the side streets and that is when it happened. It was so quick that I did not get to see anything. The street was quite quiet when I turned into it and I stepped off the pavement and ran on the road for a short distance. The next thing I hear is a car speeding up behind me. I had to dive towards the pavement and I reached it just in time, however, I was unable to remain on my feet and I crashed to the ground.

By the time I had composed myself, the car was long gone. I had no chance of getting a look at the car or registration number, let alone a glance at the driver. It may have just been a coincidence and I was just at the wrong place and the wrong time.

But somehow, I do not think so.

Friday April 22nd

After everything that happened last night, and with Petra leaving tomorrow, I decided that tonight I will let myself loose a little.

I have booked a table for Petra and I at the restaurant we had our first date at. She joked that she was only allowed out until nine o'clock tonight, whereas in truth she needs to finish packing and help Lucie get organised. I agreed to see them all before we head out to dinner (I have the table booked for seven o'clock).

After the meal, and to allow me the opportunity to forget things for a while, I have made arrangements to meet Alex, Wills, Linda and Mike at the pub. I envisage a good night ahead, hence, I am writing this at half past five having left work at four this afternoon (I thought I deserved an early finish).

So with Lars coming through tomorrow, the next diary entry should be very interesting.

Saturday April 23rd

What a night last night and what a day today.

I said my goodbyes to Lucie and wished her well and said I would look forward to seeing her in the Czech Republic one day soon. Lukas was a little quiet, so I didn't make a fuss. Petra and I had a lovely meal and she promised to call me when she arrived and would keep in touch throughout her visit.

After seeing Petra safely home, I arrived at the pub to find a slightly drunk Alex, a pretty drunk Linda, a very drunk Mike and an extremely sober Wills. I appeared to have missed out on most of the abuse that had been handed out to Wills, however, I gather that it was all in good fun and he took it well.

During the course of the evening, each of the guys confided in me over something or other and here is a run down of their current worries and concerns –

Alex – 'I am more than a little worried about the artistic direction that the movie is taking Old Boy. I think one shall have a little heart to heart with the so called director'.

Wills – ' I'm feeling good Steve, I have been working out hard for a while now so the training course should be fine but I'm still shitting myself.'

Linda – 'I'm worried about you Steve. Petra is going away, new job, losing your snooker buddy to the police. I'm worried but hey, my life is great at the moment.'

Mike – 'I'm telling you mate, it is over so it is by the way, pure O.V.E.R. I'm telling you mate, straight to Dolly Partonville for us – D.I.V.O.R.C.E. Did I tell you I am a lawyer? No, damn, that's right, I'm an accountant – and a bloody good one, but I have friends, mate, lawyer friends who will see me right.'

I left not long after midnight and walked home. I was a little worried about the state Mike was in; however, Linda was getting a taxi with him. Alex had met someone he knew and had decided to stay. Wills had left at eleven o'clock looking to get to bed as he had an early morning run planned.

I awoke alone this morning with few symptoms from the alcohol consumed last night (I must have been on better behaviour than I had planned.). I had a quick tidy of the flat before heading to meet Lars. He arrived in his traditional ripped jeans; rock t-shirt and Bronx hat (a look he has not changed for about twenty years). I noticed that he carried a briefcase the size of a suitcase with him. We agreed to drop it off at the flat before heading to the Hard Rock Café.

We managed to secure a table next to the Metallica memorabilia, much to Lars 'approval. We spent the lunch talking more about the old days, our university days and our future plans. Lars loves his job and his whole future is structured around his job. I admitted that I have no idea what my future holds and I was just living day to day at the moment.

Once I had paid for lunch, we headed back to the flat. Lars took his briefcase to the dining table and pulled out various pieces of scientific equipment to use. I brought through the notes and left them with him. From that point, he got to work and didn't speak again for another three hours.

Eventually, he looked up from some type of microscopic device and removed the gloves he had been wearing throughout. He looked at me and shook his head. No evidence could be found on the last note, no fingerprints, transfers or anything else he mentioned (he got a little technical at this point.). Nothing unusual about the ink, typeface or paper used (all appeared to have been sourced from mass produced products).

This lack of evidence did provide two major findings to Lars though.

'The perpetrator knows what they are doing Steve, and it is definitely not a hoax.'

Sunday April 24th

Petra called from the Czech Republic to confirm that they had all arrived safely, which turned out to be the highlight to a pretty awful day.

I called Dad to say that I would not be over today as I was not feeling too good. This was not a lie; however, my ailments are more mental than physical. From the moment I woke up today my head has kept repeating the same four words that Lars had said –

'...definitely not a hoax.'

When Lars left last night to go back through to Glasgow, I asked him what I should do. He suggested that I let him sleep on it and he would call me in a few days. In the meantime, I have to be both careful and observant.

I have decided that to find the culprit, I need to discover the reason for these threats. What is it they say in all the crime dramas? That's right, 'Means, Motive and Opportunity'. I need to discover the middle one if I have any hope of finding out the others or indeed the culprit. I have; therefore, decided that I must investigate my own life by writing a mini autobiography which I feel would be the best place to start my investigation.

My aim is to discover why someone feels the need to threaten my life, whilst discovering a little more about myself perhaps.

Monday April 25th

At present, when I go into work it helps me switch off from the other things that are happening in my life. Following on from the day I had yesterday, today's busy day in the office turned out to be a perfect distraction for me.

Darth and I had no fewer than three meetings in her office today. The first meeting was to discuss the usual business updates, feedback from the latest directors 'meeting, etc. Much of this I am not sure I need to know, however, Darth does like to hold court and I just go along with it. The second meeting was to finalise the details of the job advertisement for the other Senior Underwriter position. The third meeting, well I'm just not too sure the reason for it to be honest. It was a little like a heart to heart, although, Darth was doing all the talking. I guess she just had a number of things she wanted to get off her chest and she seems to like me as some kind of personal sounding board. If it keeps her happy, then I am happy to play along.

When I got home this evening, having worked on quite late, I started to think about the autobiography. I was too tired to start anything, so I lay on the sofa and started to organise my thoughts. I do genuinely believe that the reason for these threats is hidden somewhere in my past, I just cannot think where. I guess it is best to start at the beginning of my life and see where it leads me.

I just hope I get there in time…

Tuesday April 26th

Another busy day at work and the advertisement is now out and available for people to see. The closing date has been set for next Friday (6th of May) and I just wonder who will apply.

Wills called to confirm that snooker is on for tomorrow night; however, it is to be our last as his training starts on Monday.

He is now really excited and keen to get started. I can't believe how quickly this has happened and I told him as much. He agreed, though he promised to fill me in tomorrow about the full story (to this point I have heard bits and pieces – mainly due to the teasing that we have all been giving him).

I have just hung up after speaking to Alex as I wanted to bring him up to speed on Lars' visit. Once more, I found myself repeating his words –

'...definitely not a hoax.'

I think, from Alex's reaction to my plan of action, he is more excited to read my autobiography that to find out the culprit. He says that he wants to read it as I write it, however, he did say it was so he could look for clues from an independent viewpoint. I never thought about that and I think it would be good for a third party to help.

Although, I still think he just wants to read all the gory details of my life so far.

Wednesday April 27th

I took a half day today and finished at one o'clock. I have decided to start the autobiography at the weekend and get this thing going once and for all. I spent some time this afternoon on my computer, cleaning up some files and making sure it was running well, as I want to type everything up as I do it. Also, that way, I can e-mail Alex what I have written for review (and probably writing critique knowing him.).

I called Mike this evening, before heading to the snooker, to see how he was after last Friday. Lucy answered and passed the phone to Mike without saying much (although she seemed more relaxed than previous calls to the house). Mike said that he was fine, however, would be avoiding alcohol for a long time. He confirmed that things are still tough at home so was focusing on his work and spending time with Lewis. He agreed to come over soon and thanked me for calling.

Wills was in good form tonight, I sensed he was letting his hair down (metaphorically of course.) for the last time; however, he remained away from the alcohol. Apparently he applied to join the police last year but there were delays in the processing of his application. He passed the early stage interviews at that time, however, there was then a recruitment freeze and he thought that was that. Shortly after he split from Kylie, he received a call confirming that they had a post and they wanted to pursue his original application (it turns out that he had scored exceptionally highly in the interviews). From there, things moved very quickly and he was offered the job with the promise of fast track to CID which is the area he wants to work in. So, for a man who has spent the last fifteen years messing around, it seems that his life in on track.

I just wish I could say the same about myself.

Thursday April 28th

We have now reached a new level with this whole sordid affair as tonight it got physical.

I finished work around seven o'clock and stopped off for a burger on the way home (a proper burger restaurant – not the fast food type). I left just after eight and headed home. I had an uneasy feeling at the restaurant that someone was watching me and I just could not shake it.

I headed in the direction of the flat and kept looking around for anyone suspicious. When I reached the main door of the apartment block I turned round to find someone standing behind me. I was about to shout at him for invading my personal space (it was definitely a 'him'), however, I then found myself lying in the doorway. I didn't catch a glimpse of his face as he had a baseball cap pulled over his eyes and he kept his head low.

I heard him run away and I picked myself up from the floor a little gingerly. He had long gone by the time I stuck my head out of the main doorway. I then noticed that the door must have been open if I had fallen through it. I discovered that the door was not locking and I now wonder how long it has been like that. I headed up to the flat and looked at the bathroom mirror to inspect the damage. The lump in my forehead was already showing, though it is not a bad injury. I think it was the shock of being struck that floored me rather than the strike itself.

I composed myself with a stiff drink and called Lars but he was not at home and his mobile went to voice mail. I considered calling the police; however, I want to speak to Lars before I do anything further.

I just hope he will know what I should do now.

Friday April 29th

I called Darth this morning and told her I would not be in today as I could not face going to work for two reasons. Firstly, the lump on my head may start people asking questions and secondly, the latest note arrived last night. It said –

'How is your head Stephen? You could have been killed, but your time was not last night. It is soon though.'

I managed to reach Lars on his mobile this morning to tell him. He was at work and could not talk, so agreed to call me tomorrow as he is out tonight. He has some advice for me and will tell me all tomorrow. I confirmed to him that I took the same precautions with this note as I did with the last one.

Alex phoned me in the evening after I had spent the day lounging around feeling sorry for myself. I brought him up to speed and I could sense that he was upset at the news.

'I guess this latest incident proves your theory, Old Boy, that this is no longer a mere childish attempt to insert the jittering nerves into your soul.'

I guess not.

Saturday April 30th

The swelling on my forehead has reduced somewhat this evening and there appears to be little bruising. Petra called this morning and it was nice to get a diversion to the current goings on. Lucie has settled back into their old house which she had kept when she moved over to Edinburgh to be with Petra and Lukas. Lukas is fine and he has met some friends who are helping him get up to speed with his Czech, albeit, now said with a thick Edinburgh accent. I am missing Petra; however, her not being here is maybe better under the circumstances. I do now worry about her and what I am to do when she comes back as I don't want her or especially Lukas to be in any danger.

Lars called this evening and asked how I was. I explained that it was more shock than actual injury that had affected me. He said that he has spoken, in confidence, to his friend (the Detective Inspector) and made him aware of the situation and what had happened today. With Lars' confirmation that it was no longer a hoax, the inspector suggested that I call him on his mobile and he will come to the flat to speak to me in person. Lars also wants to come over again to Edinburgh and agreed to call me again to arrange this. Until then, I must make the arrangements for the police visit.

For in a few days 'time, 'An Inspector Calls'.

Sunday May 1st

I spent about five hours today working on the autobiography before heading over to Dads mid-afternoon. Writing my memoires is a bit of a strange experience, I must admit, and it was hard to think of what to write down and what to leave out. The very early years are uneventful and more about my parents moving to Edinburgh before I was born. I have completed up to the end of my primary schooling and this part of my life, I now realise, was pretty straight forward. I enjoyed primary school enormously and had a good life then.

Dad and Mary are both well and I can tell they are enjoying each others company. Mary made the most fantastic Sunday roast dinner and it was just what I needed as, if truth be told, I have not eaten well since the attack. The swelling on my head has now gone and the little amount of bruising left is covered by my hair, so it is not an issue.

I found myself to be a lot more observant on my walk home tonight and I also changed my normal route. This got me thinking again about the attack and how it has affected me. I think that it was a warning shot more that anything and I am now seriously thinking about death and being killed. After the attack I must have been in shock and I was not too sure how to handle it. It is only now, a few days later, that I know my life is truly in danger.

And that thought scares me no end.

Monday May 2nd

I have taken the week off from work, as once more my holidays are mounting up. Darth was happy with this when I called this morning and I told her that I wanted to be back in time to review the job applications with her. I do, however, feel sorry for the two teams this week as Darth has cancelled her trip to London to look over them.

At around ten o'clock I called the mobile number that Lars had given me and spoke to Inspector Edward McCreedy for the first time. He told me that Lars had filled him in and he would do what he could to help. He promised to come round on Wednesday and collect the notes as evidence and take an official statement. I could tell that he is fond of Lars by the way he spoke about him and I understand that Lars feels the same about Ed (as he refers to him).

I decided to spend the afternoon working on the autobiography. I finished my early years of high school and e-mailed them off to Alex. Again, I cannot find anything in these years that would point to such a grudge being held over me, especially all these years later. I worked pretty hard at school in the first three years and made a number of good friends. I can't remember ever having an enemy at this time, although, later this week I will revisit the remainder of my high school for such a clue.

Tuesday May 3rd

I decided to meet Linda at lunchtime today and join her for her usual walk. She decided to take an extended lunch and we walked from her office at Charlotte Square to an Italian restaurant in the Grassmarket.

She seemed in a good mood and admitted that although her personal life is complicated, she was in a 'good place'. Work is going really well for her and having reduced her long hours, she feels that she is much more productive and has been getting the results to prove this.

I was more interested in the developments of her personal life, although, she was not for giving up any information at this time. Linda and I have always confided in one another, however, when she starts a new relationship she keeps the details close to her chest. I think this is due to the times she has been hurt in the past and I always hope that any new relationship turns into the one she deserves. As such, I am happy to wait until she is ready to tell me more.

And with the secret that I am currently keeping from her, I can't do much else.

Wednesday May 4th

I met the proverbial 'Good Cop/Bad Cop' in person today when Detective Inspector McCreedy and Detective Sergeant Stone arrived at my flat this morning.

DI McCreedy was warm and comforting towards me and tried to reassure me that he would do everything in his power to get to the bottom of this situation. DS Stone, on the other hand, just asked me questions and went about his business. He didn't seem to accept that I knew of no one who wanted to harm me or who held a grudge. I tried to assure him that I really could not think of anyone.

The notes were placed into evidence bags and taken to the car by DS Stone, which gave DI McCreedy and I time to talk alone. He requested that I keep Lars' findings to myself as he didn't want to jeopardise Lars' position or the investigation. I, of course, am happy to oblige. He offered what appeared to be an apology for DS Stone and confirmed that I should not take it personally as he was always like that but he is a good officer and he wouldn't want to work with anyone else.

When he left I wondered whether they ever reversed the Good Cop/Bad Cop routine, however, I cannot see either of them in the other role.

Thursday May 5th

I worked all day on the autobiography and can't believe that I am at the end of my high school years already. I was quite bright at school and a good worker which showed in my grades. I also had a good circle of friends; however, I may have found my first potential suspect.

Chris Jackson and I were good friends up until our sixth year. We had a major falling out just before our final exams and it was, inevitably, over a girl. At a pre-exam party, the girl in question was a little drunk and I was a little more than drunk. I seem to recall that Chris was on holiday with his parents at the time and the girl (who Chris had been dating for a month or so) began hitting on me.

Now, I know that I should have been in better control of myself but one thing led to another and we got together. When Chris returned from holiday and found out that he had been traded for me, he confronted me, floored me with a single punch and swore never to speak to me again. I knew that the exams were important for his university plans (I had already secured my place having done well in Fifth year) and I never did find out what happened. Needless to say the girl and I only lasted a fortnight; however, my friendship with Chris was finished.

I e-mailed the latest update to Alex along with my thoughts on Chris. I cannot think of anything else that happened in those high school years that would lead to this current situation. I'm not even sure if Chris held a grudge or whether he still would after fifteen or so years. And if he did, why has he waiting until now?

Petra called today and I realised that I had not thought much about her. I hope that is a reflection on my current situation rather than a reflection of my feelings towards her. She said that Lucie is settling well into the house and Lukas was also happy. He has been spending all his spare time with some friends he has made in the neighbourhood and has been speaking non-stop in Czech. Petra stated that she is delighted, and amazed, how quickly and how well he has gotten back into the language. She said that she has had a nice time also and has even managed to catch up with some of her own friends that she has not seen for a long time.

I hung up the phone and sat in silence for a while just thinking. I just can't understand just what the hell is happening to me right now.

Friday May 6th

I have a welcome diversion today – it is Alex's birthday. Not one to shy away from a day of undiluted attention; we are all invited to his flat for a party. Alex has a fantastic flat in the New Town and his parties are famous throughout Edinburgh. He also makes a point of inviting all his neighbours so to prevent complaints about the noise.

Now the first point of note for a party at Alex's is dress code; black tie. All except Alex, of course, who will indulge himself in the wearing of a velvet or satin suit with various accessories to complete the look. I suspect a pocket watch, some style of formal headwear and a cane or umbrella. I will stick to my trusted dinner suit.

The order of the day at Alex's party is threefold –

1 – Drink. Champagne is the only drink available, with the exception of sparkling mineral water for any non-drinkers and recovering alcoholics (with many of Alex's friends being recovering artists and actors). No one is allowed to bring any other type of drink to the flat.

2 – Music. Alex has the most amazing Gramophone and a huge collection of records. The usual rule is nothing is to be played that was recorded after 1940.

3 – Conversation. Alex loves to hold an audience and will have debate and critique throughout the evening.

I have bought him a new cravat as a present and I just don't want to recall how much I paid for it, however, when in comes to Alex he is worth every penny.

Saturday May 7th

What a night, and what a morning.

As I stated, Alex's parties are legendary and last night was no exception. As expected he wore a new velvet suit, although, I'm not sure that I can quite describe the colour. It was not really pink and too light to be purple or even lilac. I guess salmon is as close as I am going to get with the description. He loved his cravat and immediately wore it. I'm not sure that the Paisley Pattern design exactly went with the suit, though, Alex was able to carry it off.

All the gang were there including PC Wills (as he is now referred to) who has a weekend at home. He is enjoying training so far and has adapted to the early morning rises. He stuck to drinking the mineral water all evening and was looking well. I also noticed that he was getting the usual attention from the fairer sex.

Except Linda, of course, who I noticed arrived unattached. She seemed in good spirits, a lot of which may have been down to the Champagne that she has a taste for. I made an indirect mention of the new man and she just smiled and said —

'It's a little complicated, Steve'.

Mike was also having a good time. We stayed off the marital subject at the party as I could tell he was tired and just wanted a good night. Going by his early consumption of the Champagne, this was obvious.

I had my fair share of the good stuff too, however, decided to leave relatively early. PC Wills left just before me and I decided to get a taxi to my flat. Although not a far distance I felt a little tipsy and, with the memories of the last attack still fresh in my head, I decided that it would be the safest option.

I was awoken at seven o'clock this morning with banging on my front door. Although my head was a little fuzzy, I had enough wits about me to react. I grabbed my jeans and jumper and slipped on my running shoes. As I headed to the door, I realised I didn't have any protection so I grabbed a knife from the kitchen. When I reached the door I noted that I need to get a spy hole and chain for my door and I had no idea who was on the other side. Gripping the knife handle a little tighter, I slowly opened the door slightly as a drunken Mike collapsed through my doorway.

'Did you know that your front door's knackered? Good job though, as I forgot what buzzer was yours.'

I helped him to his feet and allowed him to collapse again on my sofa. I said nothing as I returned the knife to the kitchen and put the kettle on to make a strong coffee. By the time I returned to the living room, Mike was mumbling to himself then started to speak a little clearer when he saw me.

'It's over now, Steve, chucked out of my own house. I can't believe it but it's my own fault. Stupid, plain stupid I have been. Why did I do it? Why there? Of course, I would get caught.'

And at that he passed out once again and I realised that my Saturday was over. It is now one o'clock in the afternoon and with Mike still on the sofa, snoring off the alcohol, I thought I would take the time to write up my entry.

Lord knows what the rest of the day will bring.

Sunday May 8th

Mike eventually rose at around two o'clock yesterday afternoon and after a strong coffee and some plain toast was full of apologies. He told me he knew that the marriage was over but having spent so long with Lucy, he was still coming to terms with it. He said that it was time to move on now and asked if I could put him up for a short while. He has a flat in Morningside and has already made arrangements with the tenants to end the agreement, but they do not move out until Friday. I said that he was welcome to stay until then.

I asked him about what he said last night about being stupid and getting caught, however, he said he could not remember what he was talking about. By the look on his face I could tell he was not being truthful, however, I didn't push the matter as I know he will tell me in his own time. I was in two minds whether to let him know about the threats but in his current situation I decided to leave it be for now. Of course, if something happens this week the issue may be forced.

I called Dad to cancel the Sunday visit and explained to him about Mike. I agreed to pop round to see him tomorrow after work for a late supper instead. Mike made a phone call to Lucy and agreed to collect some of his things this afternoon. She was taking Lewis to visit her mother, however, she told him to be gone by six o'clock. Once again I find myself helping my friend out as we loaded up his car with as much of his things we could manage (mostly work related items and clothes).

I now feel that a week of counselling lies ahead of me.

Monday May 9th

Mike awoke early and had showered, changed and made my breakfast before I had arisen. He is still remorseful at dumping himself at my door; however, I assured him that our circle of friends would always stick together.

He left as I ate and plans to work late for most of this week so has agreed to feed himself, although, he does want to take me out for dinner on Friday as a thank you. I guess his current plan is to throw himself into his work as he figures out what to do next.

I returned to work to find that there were no disasters whilst I was away. Darth met me with no real feedback regarding the teams 'performance, so I assume that they behaved themselves during the week. She did, however, run me through the applications for the Senior Underwriter post and I was pleasantly surprised to see that three of my team had applied. One will be lucky to get an interview (if I am being brutally honest), another will definitely get an interview (although I am not entirely convinced she would get the job) and the other is Sue. She has only been with us for a few months; however, she is already one of the strongest performers in my team. It may have come a bit early for her, but she has the skills and correct attitude for the role. I agreed to fully review the applications and meet with Darth tomorrow to discuss (and no doubt agree with her choices.).

Tuesday May 10th

Dad and Mary are doing well and I enjoyed my late supper with them last night. Both were in a really good mood and Dad won all three games of chess (much to the amusement of Mary I might add.). I got home at just before ten o'clock as Mike was planning to retire for the night. He has had a busy day at work and had already eaten so I said my goodnights and headed for my room (being a bit tired myself).

Petra called from the Czech Republic as I was about to start today's entry. She was due to fly back on Saturday; however, she has decided to stay an extra two weeks. She has invited me over and I am seriously considering a few days away from Edinburgh. I want to help Darth get the Senior Underwriters appointment in place first.

We had agreed to interview four candidates initially, however, we received twelve applications which were more than we had expected. After some discussion and debate we agreed to interview five. Darth and I both agreed on four names straight away, however, I suggested that we should also interview Sue.

I could tell Darth was reluctant at first, however, she did agree that she submitted a strong application. The five interviews are to take place over Thursday and Friday with a view to appointing early next week.

With that all agreed, I will arrange another week off starting 23rd of May and try and get a flight to the Czech Republic.

Wednesday May 11th

With the time off work confirmed today, I will shortly review the flights available to the Czech Republic. We also confirmed the five interview with three taking place tomorrow and the other two on Friday. I spent much of today working with Darth on the preparations of the interviews. For all her flaws, Darth is good to work with in situations such as this. She is very efficient and because we get on well enough in the working environment as people, it tends to work very well.

With all the focus on the interview, it has helped keep my mind off the other things – the threats, Petra, Mike. There is not much I can do about the threats at present except remain vigilant and cautious. My relationship with Petra will become clearer when I visit the Czech Republic. I am looking forward to seeing her again as I have missed her and our walks together. We probably have not spoken as much as we should have over the last couple of weeks, though I think it may have been harder had we spoken every day.

Mike is still working and it is now well after nine o'clock as I write this. I have not seen much of him this week; however, I think that was his intension. I guess he will sort himself out and I can only give him some space and support as required.

Thursday May 12th

The first three interviews are complete and all went well for the candidates. Out of my team, Claire was interviewed today and Sue is being seen tomorrow. Claire did exceptionally well, much better than I expected and she probably shaded the other two interviewees. Darth actually agreed with me, so I would say that she is the front runner at present, although, Darth and I will discuss them all in more detail tomorrow once the interviews are complete.

I arrived home at around seven o'clock and Mike was not in from work. I made a quick snack then headed to my room to book flights to the Czech Republic. I fly out on the morning of Monday 23rd returning late on Friday 27th. I called Petra to let her know and she sounded delighted I was coming. She has agreed to meet me at the airport and show me around Prague before heading to Lucie's. During the conversation she told me that she was not sure when she would be heading back to Edinburgh herself, I think she wants Lukas to spend more time in the Czech Republic.

I heard Mike arrive back when I was talking to Petra and, when I hung up; he was talking on his phone. I don't think he realised that I was in my room as when I came out he hung up very quickly. I never heard much of the conversation, however, I heard him say,

'I can't tell him yet, maybe after Friday…'

I could tell by the look on his face that he was talking about me, but I decided to leave it. I offered up some dinner, however, he said he had already eaten. Instead, we sat down with a beer to watch some football on the television.

Nether of us are particularly interested in football, however, it presented a necessary distraction until I headed off to bed.

Friday May 13th

I'm not superstitious (or so the Europe song goes), however, I must confess to being more than a little on edge today with it being Friday the 13th. Fortunately, as I write, nothing has happened in relation to the threats.

Darth and I completed the interviews today. Once again both candidates performed extremely well, however, I must say that Sue absolutely nailed it. Even Darth commented on how well she performed and how right I was suggesting she be interviewed. We agreed to consider them all over the weekend and make a final decision on Monday of whom to appoint.

To his word, Mike took me out for dinner tonight to thank me for putting him up (or putting up with him?). I found at the restaurant that I quite suddenly found myself quite exhausted, and unable to make more than small talk. If I am being honest, I am not sleeping well at present and have not since the attack. Mike decided not to drink tonight as he is up early tomorrow to move into his flat. I only had a couple of beers as these were only compounding my tiredness.

I have agreed to help Mike tomorrow, so I am not off for another night of restless sleep.

Saturday May 14th

Well, that's Mike away now and I have the place to myself once again. Mike was no trouble, and I was happy to help out. We moved the stuff he had into his flat and I was surprised to see how clean and tidy it was considering it has been rented out for the last few years.

I decided to have the rest of the day in my own flat and put the time to good use by having a major clean and clear out. I considered going back to my autobiography, though I ended up deciding to do that tomorrow. I will, however, take it to bed and read over what I have written thus far.

I called Petra this evening and she seemed in good spirits. She said that she is really excited and can't wait for me to come over. Lukas is also excited and they have a number of trips already planned for me. I told her that I was also really looking forward to coming.

When I came off the phone, however, two things struck me straight away –

1 – Why am I not feeling as excited as them?
2 – Why do I suddenly feel more vulnerable to these threats?

Sunday May 15th

I received a call from Lars this morning to see how I was. I confirmed that there had been no further incidents since the police had became involved. He said that that was a good sign, but to let DI McCreedy know of anything out of the ordinary. We agreed that we should meet up again some time, however, maybe better to wait until I return from the Czech Republic.

I went to see Dad as usual and all is well with him. It is great to see him so settled and happy. I genuinely think that this is the happiest I have seen him since mum died. Mary is a very different person to mum; however, she does share the same kindness and thoughtfulness that my mum showed. I told them about my trip to the Czech Republic and they asked me to pass on their regards to them all.

I headed home, noting that once again I changed my route and remained overly observant. I didn't see anything suspicious tonight – or it could be that my paranoia is subsiding (although I'm not convinced of this.)

As planned, I continued with my autobiography and may have stumbled upon potential suspect number two. I had a gap year after school before I headed to university and decided to travel. I spent the first six months in Europe – France, Spain, Italy and Greece mainly before heading to New Zealand and Australia. I spent a month in New Zealand before I flew over to Sydney. Up to this point, I had travelled alone, did not befriend anyone and was perfectly happy. When I arrived in Sydney, I met a guy called Hugo Ronson which changed the rest of the trip.

Hugo was well over six foot tall and played lots of sports. His Dad was originally from Edinburgh and Hugo had visited the city in numerous occasions. We met at a sports bar when I asked him for directions to my hotel. He recognised my accent and we got talking. After I had spent a few nights at the hotel, Hugo invited me to stay with him at his parent's house. For the next month, we spent a fair amount of time together and we just clicked as friends. He showed me round the sights of Sydney and we hit the nightlife quite hard.

Hugo had a younger brother called Leyton who would sometimes come out with us. Hugo liked to have a beer or 2, but he was a sports freak and kept himself in good shape so would rarely overdo it. Leyton, however, was much more the party animal. One weekend, Hugo travelled to a training camp with his football team and Leyton and I headed out. At this point I liked a drink, but after travelling (and drinking) for seven or eight months I suddenly wanted more. We went to a nightclub where I was offered some drugs in the toilet and, in my drunken state; I accepted and went to find Leyton. Up to this point, I had never tried drugs (that particular problem was to come later). Leyton, not surprisingly, was up for trying out my purchase and we left the nightclub to get high down by the harbour. We stayed out all night and did not return to the house until the following afternoon (Leyton also lived with his parents).

Needless to say, the whole episode did not go down well with Leyton's parents and I decided to leave the next day. I left my contact details for Hugo and headed to Melbourne. I ended up only staying a couple of weeks before deciding to head home early. My one off experience with drugs during that trip remained that – a one off.

When I arrived home, I had a letter waiting for me from Australia. I opened it up and could not believe what I was reading. It was from Hugo and it was not pleasant. It stated that Leyton had been caught in a nightclub with drugs and arrested by the police. He admitted that he was now using regularly and he confirmed that it started that night with me. The letter went on to say that I should not write back or try and contact any of the family.

It is strange to think that, all these years later, I had forgotten about the whole incident. Did something else happen to Leyton? Is Hugo now making his revenge? Is Hugo now living in Edinburgh? (He did talk about moving here one day).

I ended the evening by sending my updated writing to Alex for his comments.

Monday May 16th

And the job goes to Sue.

Darth was very impressed with her interview and how quickly she has learned the role. I was surprised that Darth is comfortable appointing someone so inexperienced, however, Darth said that she had full confidence in her and would be 'personally taking her under her wing'. Sue has learned as much in the last month as most of the team have learned in the last few years. She is always first in within the team and rarely leaves before anyone else. As sorry as I feel for Claire, and the other candidates, Sue very much deserves the appointment.

Alex rang me at dinner time to discuss the latest entry. He thinks that Hugo would be a farfetched suspect, unless he is now living in Edinburgh, something further has happened to his brother and he maintains the blame still lies with me. He also thought Chris was an unlikely suspect, although, a grudge can raise its ugly head at anytime. There may have been an incident that sparked old memories.

He concluded the conversation in congratulating me on my writing.

'We will make a writer out of you yet, Old Boy, and then you will be fully immersed in my world of the arts'

And with that, I headed to my monthly meeting…

Tuesday May 17th

The candidates were informed of the outcome today and I was pleasantly surprised how well Claire took the news. I could tell that she was disappointed; however, to her credit she commented that she thought Sue was a good choice and she is aware of how well and how hard she works.

I received a call from DI McCreedy this evening asking if anything else had happened since we last met. I stated that there had not been anything untoward and he confirmed that there was nothing further to report at his end. I told him I was heading away next week and he said the break would do me good.

I just hope he is right on that one.

Wednesday May 18th

'What is the weather like in the Czech Republic during May?'

I found myself asking this question aloud today to no one in particular in my empty flat. They say that talking to yourself is the first sign of madness, however, I think I am way beyond that already.

I decided to do an online shop for some new clothes, I can't face a clothes buying trip even if Linda was there to guide me. I decided to order a variety of new clothes for varying weather conditions from the one retailer. I just hope it all arrived before Saturday.

Thursday May 19th

I received a nice call from PC Wills tonight. He is due some time off in a couple of weeks and is desperate for a game of snooker. I joked that I thought he had forgotten about all his old mates and would be hanging out with his fellow PC Shiny Buttons. Joking aside though, I can tell that he is really enjoying things so far and I truly hope that it all works out for him. I can also admit to missing our weekly snooker games and I think that it would also be a good time to discuss these threats.

Wills, above most people in my life, deserves a break now. I know him better than most people and I know that under the confident, outgoing persona lies a very insecure, vulnerable person. I realise now that by joining the police, he was looking to combat these issues.

And right now, I know exactly how he feels.

Friday May 20th

I tidied up a few things at work today before heading off to start my week off. Sue will start her new role when I return to work on Monday 30th (under the watchful eye, as well as the wing, of Lord Vader.). I realised that I shall be required to appoint a replacement for Sue, something I am not looking forward to given the success of the last round of interviews.

I fancied going out tonight for a drink, so I called round some of the guys. I knew Wills was still at training and Alex is working on some writing but he wants to meet up next week to hear all about the Czech Republic. Mike and Linda are both busy tonight as well, so I find myself facing an early night tonight.

I suppose the rest may do me some good.

Saturday May 21st

I was relieved to receive a package this morning of my online purchases. The clothes pretty much fit well, although I may have lost a little weight as the trousers are a little looser than normal (I wonder if this is down to my healthier or more stressful lifestyle). I decided to clean up the flat and get everything organised for the trip. I duly packed up my case before heading down to the bank to collect some currency.

The city centre was busy as the tourist season appears to have begun early. Amongst the usual groups of Hen and Stag party goers (and it is not yet noon.) the first requests for directions has begun. I must have one of those faces that says 'Sure, I can give directions. Yes, no problem I will take your photo with the castle in the background'.

It was much more fun, though, in the days before digital cameras with their instant results. In those days, I could at least enjoy the thought of the happy tourists developing their photos with the castle sticking directly out of the top of their head.

Sunday May 22nd

Another note came today whilst I was out. I had only been gone for around forty minutes (I had a few toiletries to purchase) and when I came back it was there waiting for me.

I called DI McCreedy and he asked me not to touch it (which I hadn't) and he would come round. He arrived within the hour and I was surprised to see him dressed in a rock t-shirt and jeans. He noticed my glance and apologised for his clothes, however, he was currently off duty. As he lived locally, he was happy to come round to help though. He put on gloves and carefully opened the note before placing it in an evidence bag. Safely sealed, he passed the note for me to read.

'Not with a knife, nor a gun, yet a life you did destroy'

I simply shook my head as it made no sense to me. I passed the note back to DI McCreedy who thanked me for calling him and left for the police station. Of all nights, I did not want to be thinking about this before I head to the Czech Republic.

And despite my early flight in the morning, I sense another restless night awaits me.

Monday May 23rd

I slept more than I thought I would by focusing on seeing Petra again rather than on the note.

The flight both left and arrived on time and Petra stood waiting for me at arrivals. She ran to me and we immediately embraced and as I held her I felt and heard her sobs. I pulled back slightly after a while and looked into her moist eyes. Before I could ask, she was shaking her head saying it was so good to see me.

Despite my load of pre trip purchases, I ended up packing light and I was glad of this given the day Petra had planned. She took me round the main sights of Prague – Prague Castle, Charles Bridge; the old town (sounds about like Edinburgh does it not?). She also booked a table at her favourite restaurant which was just delightful. The weather was kind to us also, dry and pleasant without being overly hot.

As we sat on the evening bus to her home town, I realised that all the strong feelings I have for her have returned. I can only imagine that my reservations related to everything else that has been happening in my life and not related to Petra.

We arrived late to the house at which point Lukas was already sleeping. Lucie had waited on my arrival and was looking fabulous. We had a catch up and I passed on my Dad's regards over a cup of tea. Lucie headed for bed and I was shown to my room to unpack. I notice that the room has a double bed and lots of Petra's things. I decided to write today's entry whilst she is currently in the shower.

And I hope that she will shortly be joining me…

Tuesday May 24th

I was awoken this morning by a very cheerful Lukas who was playfully jumping up and down on the end of the bed. I noticed that Petra must have arisen earlier as she came through, fully dressed, with a cup of coffee for me. When I looked at the clock on the bedroom wall I noticed that it was half past eleven. Even allowing for the time difference with Scotland, I realised that I had just had the best night's sleep in weeks.

After changing, and having a very late breakfast, we decided to spend the day in Petra's town. Petra has plans for the remainder of the week so I guess she just wanted to ease me in gently. Lucie had a few things to do so the three of us went for a walk. The town is beautiful and the sun decided to come out to greet me also. Lukas was excited to show me round the place and Petra was happy to let him take the lead.

We headed back home for dinner and Lucie had it all prepared to her usual high standard. We sat round the table for a few hours talking about Czech customs and they even tried to teach me some of the language, which I am truly useless at.

Admitting defeat, I helped get Lukas to bed before Petra and I listened to some music before heading of to bed together again.

Wednesday May 25th

We spent much of today on Czech buses as we visited some of Petra's relatives. Czech buses are an institution in themselves. Firstly, they are exceptionally clean and tidy. Secondly, they are very comfortable to travel in. Finally, they are beyond punctual. If a bus is due to leave the station at ten o'clock, the driver will get behind the wheel at 9:59, start the engine and when his clock turns to ten o'clock he will shut the doors and drive off.

I think our rail network needs a Czech in charge.

Thursday May 26th

It is my last full day in the Czech Republic before I head home tomorrow. I had a day visiting more relatives today and had a thoroughly good time. Petra has a crazy uncle who I met today. He does not speak a work of English; however, we spent the whole afternoon in floods of tears laughing with each other.

Petra and I have decided to spend tomorrow in Prague together before my late afternoon flight. She has booked the same restaurant for lunch tomorrow and suggested that this would give us the chance to talk together.

I have really enjoyed myself here and I am a little disappointed that I chose to stay for the five days only. All of Petra's family have invited me back, so maybe it will not be too long until I come back over again.

Friday May 27th

It is now half past eleven at night; I am back in Edinburgh and thoroughly knackered.

Petra and I has a great time again in Prague where we visited a museum and art gallery. We had our lunch as planned and took the time to talk things over. I guess what she told me did not come as a complete surprise; I sensed it during our phone calls, although I did not admit it to myself.

Petra is staying in the Czech Republic.

Her decision revolves mainly around Lukas who wants to stay. It transpires that he was being bullied by some of his classmates back in Edinburgh and, despite the best efforts of the school; it has been getting progressively worse. He visited the local school for a few days last week and fitted in instantly. The lease on Petra's flat in Edinburgh expires next month and she has decided not to renew it. She has also been offered a good job in Prague.

Sitting in the restaurant, hearing what she had to say, I had to explore my feelings quickly. Selfishly, I want her and Lukas back in Edinburgh. Realistically, I want what is best for them both. I asked what would happen with 'us' and she said that she wanted 'us' to stay 'us'. I was welcome to visit anytime, she could come over to Edinburgh sometimes during the year and we could see how things went. This was exactly what I wanted to hear.

On the flight home I came to the conclusion that this was the best option for all parties involved. Lukas and Petra could

151

settle back in the Czech Republic, I could get some cheap flights from Edinburgh to Prague and we could see each other every month or two, even if just for a long weekend. Also, with everything else that is going on, it would ensure their safety.

Truth be told, if anything happened to Petra or Lukas I just wouldn't be able to go on.

Saturday May 28th

I met with Linda today to discuss my trip. She was visibly upset that Petra is staying in the Czech Republic and made me promise to get her over to Edinburgh again for a visit. I told her that Petra would be coming over next month to empty the flat so I would arrange a get together then.

I asked how she was doing and she confirmed that she is great. Work is fantastic; she is maintaining reasonable hours and getting so much done. Her love life is getting better, but does not want to jinx it yet. She is also looking forward to seeing PC Wills next week as she has missed him and his stories.

I headed home late having seen Linda home. I noticed that the main door to the flat had been fixed at last.

I just wonder if that will also be the end of these bloody notes.

Sunday May 29th

I spent the whole day with Dad and Mary today. I decided to take them out for dinner rather than have them cook for me.

It was good to see them, out together, in a neutral venue and they certainly came across as the happy couple. I wonder if they plan to marry one day, or if they are just happy in each other's company.

Whatever they decide, I am delighted for them both.

Monday May 30th

Sue started her new job today and Darth was spending much of the day fussing over her. I wonder how long my 'Blue Eyed Boy' status will remain. Sue seemed at ease in the role as I witnessed this first hand when Darth asked me to sit in on her first team meeting. She handled it with supreme professionalism.

PC Wills called this evening and we have agreed to meet up for snooker on Wednesday (like the old days.) and all five are meeting up on Friday.

It should be a good week.

Tuesday May 31st

And I spoke too soon.

Alex was attacked tonight.

I received the call at half past eight this evening telling me he had been taken to hospital. I ran out of the flat, hailed a taxi almost immediately and arrived at the hospital within twenty minutes of the call.

Fortunately, Alex is going to be fine but I could tell he got one hell of a fright. His right eye is badly swollen and he has some cuts on the side of his face. His body is also covered with bruises; however, no bones have been broken. Alex was putting on a brave face waiving the affair off as being the responsibility of some 'educationally deprived, socially inept, alcoholically induced Glaswegian'.

When I stepped out of the hospital (he is being kept in overnight for observations) I started to cry. In fact, I was doubled over in some sort of wailing, sobbing fit. It took me a good fifteen minutes to compose myself as the Edinburgh public hurried past me pretending I was not there. It could, of course, be a coincidence that Alex was attacked tonight. I, however, do not believe in such coincidences and can not help to think that it is related to me.

And for some reason, I am wholly responsible.

Wednesday June 1st

I booked a holiday from work as I could not face going into the office today. I also needed to call the hospital and speak to D.I. McCreedy about Alex's attack.

When I called the hospital, the nurse confirmed that Alex's physical injuries are fine and he was being let out this morning. They did not comment on his psychological injuries, and I chose not to ask. I was put through to Alex who started talking with his usual great bravado before surprising me.

'The thing is Old Chap, well, one is a little shook up you see and I was wondering if you would do yours truly the honour of allowing me to spend a few nights at Apartamento Hamilton '

Alex is; of course, welcome to stay here as long as he wishes, however, my concerns about the attack being related to me made me hesitate. In the end, I suggested that he stay and I would take the rest of the week off work and stay with him.

I called D.I. McCreedy before I left to meet Alex from hospital. He agreed that Alex would be better staying with me, but recommended extra vigilance. He also confirmed that he would come to the flat tomorrow to interview Alex and talk to me.

I met Alex at the hospital and we got a taxi to his flat to collect some of his things before heading over to mine. I called Wills and suggested that he come over rather than head out for snooker.

When Wills arrived I hugged him. It is not the normal thing we do when we meet each other and I guess I took him by surprise, however, when he looked at Alex on the sofa he understood. I spent the next hour or so telling Wills about the threats and how I thought Alex's attack may be related. I could tell he was shocked and he did question me why I didn't tell him sooner. After my explanation, he understood and was very supportive. So much so, he went home and returned an hour later with some things and a sleeping bag.

Apartamento Hamilton has just turned into a Guest House.

Thursday June 2nd

Despite the circumstances, we all had an enjoyable evening together as Wills filled us in on his training and shared some stories. I let Alex sleep in my bed due to his current state as Wills and I fought over who gave up the sofa and slept on the floor (I won – I need to look after my guests).

D.I. McCreedy and D.S. Stone came round at lunchtime and I introduced them both to Alex and Wills. The Good Cop/Bad Cop routine started straight away, I'm not sure it ever stops right enough. The main points of the attack were –

1 – Alex was taken by complete surprise and the attack was not provoked.
2 – It happened in a darkened area and he did not see who was responsible.
3 – He could not confirm if it was one attacker or a group.
4 – He did not hear, see or smell anything that would help.
5 – The police did not have much to go on.

When asked if anything had been stolen, Alex confirmed that it was only his phone that was taken. D.I. McCreedy concurred with me that it sounded more like an attack than a robbery. If it had been a robbery, why did they not take his money or wallet? D.S. Stone was not so sure though, he noted that the phone that was taken was a valuable, sought after phone. Also if it was an attack, why take the phone at all?

Once the interview was concluded, both officers spoke to Wills about how his training was going and they shared some of their own stories from when they completed theirs. It was refreshing to see Wills speak to them in such a professional manner and I can tell that he will make an excellent police officer. I could see that he was keen to make a good impression and D.I. McCreedy left his contact details with Wills and told him to call him anytime he wanted any advice. I discovered later that Wills has aspirations of working in CID.

And right now, it could not come quickly enough.

Friday June 3rd

I called Lars last night after writing up my entry. I told him about the attack on Alex and suggested that he come over in a couple of weeks 'time once things have settled. He told me that D.I. McCreedy was keeping him informed on the case, albeit, he was not directly involved.

Alex has perked up a bit today and to my surprise suggested that we all go ahead with the trip to the pub. Nodding towards Wills, he stated –

'One now has one's very own personal bodyguard, recently fully trained in the art and delights of close contact combat'.

So as he showers himself, and Wills heads home for a change of clothes, I thought I would write a quick entry for today.

I am just not sure at what time we will all return tonight.

Saturday June 4th

Well despite his injuries, and the mental effect the attack must have had on him, Alex was mostly his usual flamboyant self last night. He brushed off the attack as 'one of life's little inconveniences' when explaining to Linda and Mike what had happened. I specifically requested that we did not tell them about the threats as I wanted to tell them both at a suitable time.

We all had a good time and Wills spent most of the night recalling stories of his previous escapades before, in recent months, turning all sensible. Wills is always in good form when he talks about his 'wild days' (although I think 'wild years' would be more appropriate). This, of course, gave us all the perfect opportunity to tease him on his relationship with Kylie. Linda even got involved asking 'What exactly did you see in her?', 'That would be telling...' was Wills' reply.

We remained in the pub until closing time and Mike and Linda got a taxi together (Mike's flat is close to Linda's, so it makes sense). The three of us got to my flat in the early hours of this morning. Alex was self-exclaimed 'rather well lubricated', I was more than a little tipsy (as I tried to keep tonight's drinking at a sensible level) and Wills was stone cold sober.

The weather took a turn for the worst today, with torrential rain coming down all day, so we decided to stay in. We spent much of the time debating what movies to watch, what music to listen to and what carry out food to order. Wills also took control of the games console, much to Alex's dismay.

With the different stresses we are all going through at this time, I think today's events were just what we all needed.

Sunday June 5th

Wills was up early this morning as he was heading back to the Police College this afternoon. He did, however, go out to get our breakfast and some newspapers and has this all prepared for Alex and I before we woke.

Alex is feeling a whole lot better and the swelling in his eye is subsiding nicely. As such, he was happy to go back to his flat today, although, I told him he could stay over anytime and he was just to call me if he needed anything. I helped him get his things together and then walked him down to his flat before heading to Dads house.

As I walked through the city centre, I thought about everything that has happened and whether to tell Dad and Mary. I think that Dad is so contented at this time that I do not wish to over alarm him or upset him in anyway.

That said, if Alex's attack was because of me, I may not have any other choice than to tell them everything.

Monday June 6th

I went back to work today and I could tell that Sue is settling in well to her new role. I had a meeting with Darth and she spoke of how well Sue is doing. Apparently, Darth was called to a meeting on Friday so Sue was left in charge of both teams and handled the situation perfectly. Successful Sue right enough.

I finished work sharply tonight as I wanted to try and finish my autobiography. I was home by a quarter past five and I started typing straight away. It is now half past eleven and I have just finished (and trying to eat my dinner as I write this). I could not find anyone obvious in the final chapter; however, writing these notes took me back to my time with Sarah.

Before I met Petra, I had had only one serious girlfriend. I dated Sarah James for only about six months; however, we had to deal with a lot during that time. Mum had recently passed away and I was not coping well (my drug habit had started by this point). We met at a party and got on instantly, we just seemed to click. We left the party early, together, and headed to the Meadows to talk alone. Sarah's father had been tragically killed in a car accident so we could relate to each others pain and suffering. It seemed to all intents and purposes that we were made of each other.

Everything was going perfectly between us; however, my drug usage was increasing. In the end, we had a blazing row (I think it was related to my drug usage, although I cannot fully remember) and we split up. I remember at the time thinking we would soon get back together, however, she left Edinburgh for London and we never saw each other again after that. I do not think that any of this is related to the threats but I thought it was worth documenting.

If something does happen to me, and someone reads these notes, I think it should be noted that Sarah was a very special person.

And I screwed it up.

Tuesday June 7th

The main door is broken again.

I came home from work and found a group of youths hanging about the landing, sheltering from the rain (I know that it is June, but it is Edinburgh.). I did challenge them on the broken door; however, they swore it was like that when they passed.

I went into the flat and called Alex. He says that he is doing fine and had enjoyed reading the final chapter of my autobiography this morning (I had e-mailed it to him last night). He did not spot anything suspicious; however, he was interested to find out what happened to Sarah once she left for London. I remember that she graduated with a law degree and I believed that she was heading down there for a job. I knew some of her friends from Edinburgh at the time; however, they shunned me after the fall out.

Knowing Sarah, as I did back then, I am sure she landed on her feet.

Wednesday June 8th

I called the building maintenance company about the main door last night; however, I was too late. Another note arrived.

I called D.I. McCreedy to let him know. He said I could open and read the note as the chances of there being any forensic evidence was low given the tests done on the previous notes. Lars, however, had left some latex gloves when he was over so I put a pair on before opening the note and reading the content over the phone to D.I. McCreedy.

'How is your friend Steve? A problem shared in a problem halved. A threat shared is a threat doubled'

He told me to tell Alex to be extra vigilant and to report anything suspicious to him directly. He confirmed that he had given Alex his card after the interview so would have his contact details.

I can not put down in words at this time how I feel. A threat aimed at me (despite the fact I do not know the reason for this) is one thing and I can cope with this. A threat aimed at my best friend, is something completely different. If anything was to happen to him, the sender of these threats would have their work done.

I would kill myself.

Thursday June 9th

I received my first ever dressing down from Darth today. I have just not been able to concentrate on work of late and have made a few mistakes. To be fair to her, she took me into her office and spoke firmly, but fairly. I obviously could not tell her what is going on, however, I must be careful at work.

In way of compensation, I worked on late tonight, I fixed the mistakes that I had made and decided to do some auditing of the teams work. I noticed a few issues there that I will need to clear with them tomorrow. It's been a while since any of my team members have made such errors so I will need to get a hold of this before it escalates.

By the time I got home, lacking any sort of appetite, I collapsed on my bed. I will enter a long deep sleep, just as soon as I finishing writing…

Friday June 10th

Something is wrong with Linda, but I will not find out until tomorrow.

She rang me this afternoon at work in floods of tears. Every time she started to speak, she just started to cry and then hung up the phone. I phoned her back a few times, but I could not get any sense out of her. I eventually told her that I would go to her house tomorrow and spend the day with her.

I just hope that she has not been targeted like Alex was.

Saturday June 11th

If I see Mike, I swear I am going to rip him apart.

I met with Linda at her place and spent the day there with her as planned. It took a long time for the full story to come out, however, I will try and document it the best I can.

Linda and Mike have been secretly seeing each other for about nine months. At the start, it began as an affair that was not supposed to last. Things have not been good between Mike and Lucy since Lewis was born. I had no idea of this; it was only in the last few months that I noticed something was wrong. So, as things started deteriorating with Lucy, they got more serious with Linda. Linda told me that, being with Mike, she had not felt like that with someone for a long time.

Linda knew that Mike's marriage was over and that it was just a matter of time until it was official. She was in no hurry and wanted to wait until the divorce was finalised before getting more serious with Mike. They had been careful until after Alex's party when they got caught in Mike's car by Lucy. Linda knew it was bound to happen sooner or later and it, perversely, speeded up the separation.

Since Mike moved into his flat, they had been seeing more of each other. They had started planning for the future with Mike telling Linda that he felt the same. Once the divorce was finalised, they planned to live together.

This past week, Linda noted that Mike had started to act a little strangely. He started getting short with her and also shouted at her a few times. She just put it down to the stress of the pending divorce and pressure at work. Little did she realise that things would come to a head on Thursday evening.

Linda decided to surprise Mike and take him out for dinner. She went to his office, but the reception staff told her that he had already left. Linda then went to Mike's flat, but there was no reply. His phone was switched off, so she decided to get a coffee to go and wait outside the flat for him coming back. An hour or so later Mike arrived back, with a young girl on his arm. Mike obviously did not see Linda as, just before they reached the flat, he turned and passionately kissed the mystery girl.

Needless to say, Linda ran as fast as she could away, screaming. She told me that there would be no way that Mike did not hear or see her at that point. She did not look back, but could tell that he did not give chase. Mike is fitter than any of us and would have easily have caught up with her.

As fit as he is, he better stay away from me.

Sunday June 12th

I spoke with Alex this morning and told him about the most recent note and my discussions with D.I. McCreedy. I felt myself getting quite emotional telling him about the content of the note and I think he sensed this in my voice. He told me not to worry about it, although it was darn inconvenient, the attacker (or attackers) could have done much worse to him. Once again, it makes me think that the person responsible for all this is toying with me.

I find going to Dads, on a Sunday afternoon, a welcome diversion to the current situation. I must admit though that I am getting more wary about the journey to and from his house. When I arrived, Dad seemed in great spirits, as did Mary. So much so, I debated on asking them about it, however, I decided just to enjoy their company.

When I left, I found myself hailing a passing taxi cab to take me back to the flat. It was not dark and I could not see anyone around but I guess I am still a little shaken from recent events.

And I guess the driver would have been happy taking a few pounds off me on his way back to the city centre.

Monday June 13th

I took myself into work early today and decided to focus completely on my job. I spent most of my time today with the staff, following up on a meeting I had with them last Friday. With everything that happened with Linda, I did not have the chance to document that I had a very frank meeting with them. I did accept some the blame for the dropping of standards, however, I confirmed that the errors being made currently were unacceptable. I guess you could describe it as being firm, but fair.

That stated, I detect that I may be turning into a 'Mini-Darth'

Tuesday June 14th

I called Lars tonight and we have made arrangements for him to come through to Edinburgh on Saturday. I will meet him at the train station at around ten in the morning, which no doubt means an early trip to the Hard Rock Café. He said that he is keen to see the latest note, despite the reluctance of D.I. McCreedy to look at it further himself (Lars had already spoken to his colleague who is happy for him to take a look).

I also called Petra tonight and found that I am missing her terribly. I feel somewhat caught between a rock and a hard place as although I want to see her; I want her to be safe. I was able to keep my emotions in check and I do not think that she suspected anything wrong.

When she comes to Edinburgh at the end of the month, however, I am not so sure I will be able to keep up this façade.

Wednesday June 15th

Thursday June 16th

Those eagle-eyed readers will have spotted I missed my first entry of the year yesterday. And the reason – I bumped into Mike.

Well, when I say I bumped into Mike, my fist bumped into his face.

I was walking home from work when it all happened. I turned a corner not far from my flat when we met. We were both alone and I started to shout at him. He acted very defensively, saying he did not want to hurt anyone, especially not Linda. It was at that point I lost my temper and started to verbally abuse him (I cannot remember exactly what I said, but it was far from pleasant). The verbal abuse escalated to pushing and eventually I punched him square on his jaw.

To be fair to Mike, he did not retaliate, he just tried his best to block as many of my punches as he could. It was just my luck that a police car passed at that point. We were split up, handcuffed and taken to the local police station.

During the interview, I confirmed that I was solely to blame and Mike was at no fault for the fight. After signing my statement, I heard the interviewing officer tell a colleague to release Mike. I was told that I would be spending the night in the cells and that I was allowed one phone call. Of all the people I could have chosen to call, I chose Darth. I told her that I needed to take an emergency holiday for today and tomorrow.

As promised I spent the night in an uncomfortable cell, albeit, I was glad to be alone. I was awoken this morning by a grinning D.S. Stone (the first time I has seen a smile on his face) and taken to another interview room. The awaiting D.I. McCreedy stood up and told me to take a seat and he was smiling also. His smile, however, was warm in comparison to that of D.S. Stone. D.I. McCreedy confirmed that Mike did not wish to press charges and that he was happy to release me, putting the matter down to recent incidents and the stress I was currently under. He was obliged, however, to give me a warning.

I came home and tried to gather my thoughts. I have not been in a fight since I was sixteen years old and I am pretty disgusted with my behaviour. Regardless of my feelings towards Linda, this was no way to act or to deal with the situation. After having another cup of coffee (deciding that this was the better option to alcohol), I decided to call Alex and he agreed that I could go and see him tonight.

I just have the small matter of collecting £100 from the ATM on my way over.

Friday June 17th

Despite the bet being over, I have decided to try and maintain a daily entry in the diary. I am not sure if I will manage this at all times, however, I will do my best.

Alex was reluctant to accept the money from me, but a bet is a bet so I forced him to. He said that he will put the money to 'good artist usage'. I obviously gave him the full details on why I did not write the entry and about Mike and Linda. I was a little surprised when he said that he was proud of me despite his hatred of violence (which has escalated greatly following his recent attack). I also gave him a key to my safe (which I recently installed in my flat) and told him if anything happened to me he was to take the diary and any other contents in there. I am happy with this arrangement as Alex is the only person I can truly trust.

I spent today contemplating what to do about Mike. We are friends that go back a long time and he could have taken the matter further and made my life even more uncomfortable. I guess he is going through a lot himself at present with the separation; however, I will never be able to forgive him for how he treated Linda. I decided to leave things with Mike for now and called Linda instead.

I was not sure how she would react to the events of Wednesday evening, however, to my relief she actually laughed. I suppose that this was as good an outcome as I could have wished for, though once she started calling me Cassius Clay I was not so sure. Linda told me later that she is very hurt with what happened and will never be able to forgive Mike, regardless of what he is going through.

I could do little but concur.

Saturday June 18th

I have just seen Lars off at the train station with him catching the last train to Glasgow. It was another good day spent in his company.

As expected, we started off with brunch and some drinks at the Hard Rock Café (which may be the real reason for his trips to see me.). He turned up wearing a classic Deep Purple t-shirt, telling me that nothing will beat the classic rock era of the 1970's. For some strange reason, we decided to take a bus tour of Edinburgh in the afternoon. I guess it is a good way for Lars to see round the city and he seemed to really enjoy it.

When we reached my flat later on in the afternoon, I showed him the latest note. At this point, be became silent and popped open his forensic case (which he had brought again) and got to work. I left him to it and made myself a coffee (Lars did not want anything to disturb his work). Sooner than the last time, he concluded again that no trace evidence could be located. Disturbing, he said 'this guy is very, very good'. I could actually read the disappointment in his face. I then told him about my autobiography and he asked if he could read it.

I thought he would take a copy back home, however, he insisted that he read it in full. We ate dinner, as he continued to read, asking questions from time to time. His conclusion matched that of Alex and me, it could only possibly be three people. Even at that, he thought it unlikely someone would hold a grudge that long. He suggested that I try and find out what had happened to them since I last saw them. He also suggested that I tell D.I. McCreedy about them as it may help the investigation.

I will, therefore, call him on Monday.

Sunday June 19th

I think that it is fair to say that I have been through quite a lot this past year, but even so, I did not see this one coming. Dad and Mary are moving to Spain.

Mary has a house there which she bought back in the 1980's and has rented it out ever since. She has decided to sell her house in Edinburgh (which has already been arranged) and move to Spain permanently, which was always her intention when she bought the house. She asked Dad to come with her and he has agreed.

Once I got over the initial shock, I realised that I was extremely happy for them both. I have become very fond of Mary and she obviously has a greatly positive effect on Dad. They plan to move at the end of the month as the sale is going through next week.

They said that I could stay with them at any time and I think, given my current situation, it may be sooner rather than later.

Monday June 20th

I went back to work again today and I noticed that I still have over four weeks holiday to take, including a 'summer fortnight'.

I called D.I. McCreedy to discuss Lars' visit and my autobiography. He was not available today so I spoke to D.S.

Stone instead. He agreed with Lars that it would be highly unlikely that anyone would hold a grudge for that length of time and the police are looking for someone who I may have upset more recently. He stated that they are currently looking into a 'number of lines of enquiry'. It all sounded very much scripted; although he said he would pass on my message to D.I. McCreedy.

The team seem to be in good shape and Darth confirmed that things appear to be back to normal. Sue is still getting on well with the new role (and Darth.). I stayed back to nearly nine o'clock tonight on the basis that it gave me time to catch up (and I had nothing better to do tonight).

As I was leaving, however, Sue shouted good night from the other room.

Tuesday June 21st

Alex is proving to be not only a trusted friend at present, but a continuous source of diversion. Tonight he had the premier of his short film shown at the Edinburgh International Film Festival at the Filmhouse.

Given recent events, I was worried how Alex would react, and also if he would be a target. I dressed for the occasion in traditional dinner suit and was surprised to see Alex dressed in a similar fashion (it was not until later that I saw the 1920's gold pocket watch attached to his same era pattered waistcoat). From the close knit circle of friends, I was the only one in attendance. Will is still at Police College and both Mike and Linda declined their invites.

My concerns proved to be completely unfounded in both counts. There were no apparent threats on either Alex or I and Alex behaved in his usual flamboyant manner. 'I feel my most comfortable surrounded by my own remarkable and talented people' as he put it. He was truly in his element and enjoying all the attention he was receiving. The film was tremendous (in my humble option) and was well received.

The Filmhouse bar was flowing once again with Champagne when Alex arrived there after the showing.

Wednesday June 22nd

I decided to call Mike tonight, possibly against my better judgement, but I had to deal with the matter and in the end I am glad I did.

When I called, he let me do all the talking and I certainly used the time to full advantage by getting a week and a half's worth of anger and frustration out. I did not miss a thing and made my feelings perfectly clear. Mike just listened as I went on until I finished by apologising for hitting him. Regardless of what he did, violence was not the answer. He told me that it was nothing less than he deserved and that is why he did not take the matter further.

Mike told me he has been contemplating his actions and trying to work things out over the last week or so. He has accepted that he has problems that he needs to deal with and thinks a change from Edinburgh may be the answer. As such, he has decided to move to London. Lucy has told him to stay away from her and Lewis and Mike thinks that it would be best to take some time away. His firm has wanted him to help set up a new operation in London for a while and this may be a good opportunity. He is not sure how long he will be away; however, he expects to be away for at least six months.

Mike also confirmed that he has spoken to Linda and apologised for everything that happened. He knows that he will never get forgiveness, from either of us, but has hopes that we can remain in contact.

And we left it at that.

Thursday June 23rd

I called Alex this evening to see how he was getting on. He told me that he has been receiving many phone calls regarding his film and is hopeful that 'something truly remarkable and wonderful will come out of this little ditty of my making'.

He also told me that he has not received any threats and has not noticed anything suspicious since the attack; however, he was being careful and more observant of late. He also confirmed that he had re-read the autobiography and thinks that we should meet up on Saturday and start our own investigation into potential suspects.

I just hope that he will not arrive dressed as Hercule Poirot.

Friday June 24th

D.I. McCreedy called me this evening, but not in relation to the threats, he wanted to ask me about Wills.

He has made a point of calling a friend at the Police Collage to keep an eye, and report back, on the progress Wills is making. Apparently, the feedback has been extremely positive and D.I. McCreedy wanted to ask me, in confidence, some character questions.

He stated he was interested in previous 'party days' or when he went out to let his hair down. He was more interested about his mental strength and how I thought he would react in certain situations. For all Wills liked to party (and was often the life and soul of those he attended) he is one of the most intelligent, level headed people I know (despite the whole Kylie incident.). As such, my responses were both positive and truthful.

I asked D.I. McCreedy the reason for the questions and he confirmed that when he spoke to Wills recently, he had indicated to him that he would be monitoring his progress. Wills had also asked to let him know of any opportunities in CID that may arise. As it turns out, D.S. Stone is retiring at the end of November and there could be some movement within the department. If Wills continues to display his current attributes, D.I. McCreedy may try and fast track him to the department.

I am not sure if I see Wills as 'Bad Cop' though.

Saturday June 25th

Petra called last night after I had written my entry. She is flying into Edinburgh on Wednesday morning and will pack up her things then. She has a Czech removal company coming over and they are due to arrive on Wednesday night to take everything away. She said that she does not have much to pack as the flat was already furnished so it is just clothes and personal effects. She does not fly back until Friday, so we will have some time together before she goes back.

Alex came over at lunch time today and insisted on cooking a vegetarian Middle Eastern dish he had just discovered. Despite my reservations, it turned out to be very tasty indeed. He never fails to impress me does our Alex.

After lunch, we turned our attention to the three people from the autobiography. As I have previously documented, I am not really up with modern technology when it comes to the whole social networking thing. Alex, on the other hand, is an expert so once I had signed on to my Facebook account he took over.

It took us most of the day (being from so long ago it was hard to remember all the details), however, we found two out of the three people in question. Chris Jackson is married, living in Manchester and seems to be very happy. Hugo Ronson is still in Australia although we could not find Leyton. We sent friend requests to them both and will see what happens.

We did not have such luck with Sarah James, although, she could be married and have changed her name. We did, however, find one of her friends that I got well with at the time and she is still living in Edinburgh. We decided to send her a friend request also.

The waiting, therefore, begins.

Sunday June 26th

Despite checking many times during today, there were no responses to any of my 'friend' requests. As such, I continued cleaning my flat (which you never see on Detective shows).

I realised as I walked to Dads that this would be our last traditional Sunday together. It made me think of mum and how much I miss her. I do sometimes wonder what she would make of it all, if she was looking down on us all now. I am sure she would be happy that Dad was moving on and getting on with his life. I can imagine her saying 'Now, be nice to Mary and remember to change your shirt'.

I could tell that Dad had already made a start on his packing with a number of boxes taped up and ready to go. Mary has organised a removal firm to collect their things and ship them over to Spain.

As Mary was making some dinner, Dad wanted to know what I really thought. I assured him that I was very happy for him and that he should just get on and enjoy his life. He is still young enough that he should take these opportunities. I said that I would look after the house, so if it did not work out he could always come back.

I suspect from the reaction on his face when I said that, there is little chance of that happening.

Monday June 27th

Darth held a meeting this morning with Sue and me.

She wanted to go over some items from her last meeting in London with us both ensuring we were both 'kept in the loop' (I hate these expressions and Darth has a mental dictionary full of them). It was much of the same and there was nothing new in it for me. Sue, being new to the whole experience, took a copious amount of notes and asked lots of questions. This allowed Darth to extend the half hour meeting to nearly two hours.

I received a call from Mike this evening as he leaves for London tomorrow. I wished him good luck (although, I did this in a manner that told him I was still angry with him) and asked him to let me know how it goes. I realised, when I came off the phone, this is going to be a strange week. Mike, Dad and Petra are all moving away from Edinburgh this week.

If Linda decides to go, there will only be Alex left.

Tuesday June 28th

I received my first reply in relation to the investigation.

It came from Chris Jackson and was not what I expected. He sent me a note saying it was great to hear from me and that he hoped I was doing well. It also said that he was sorry for being so childish at school and that splitting up with the girl was the best thing that happened to him. After failing his exams, he took a year out and went travelling. He returned to the UK and decided to move to Manchester to do some A-Levels (he was very into the local music scene at that time). Upon passing them all, he went on to a local university where he met his now wife. They have set up an IT consultancy business which is doing exceptionally well and have three children. After reading all this, I find it difficult to suspect him of any part in this whole affair.

I headed over to see Dad and Mary off and went with them to the airport. I swear, they were acting like a couple of over-excited teenagers going on their first trip abroad. I really cannot believe the difference in Dad this past year. He has turned from a quiet gentleman trying to fill his days (mostly at the bowling club), to a confident, happy individual ready to live his life to the full.

I just hope I can do the same.

Wednesday June 29th

I arranged more time off work to be with Petra. She arrived on the early morning flight from Prague.

We had some quick brunch then headed to her flat to pack. She had asked me to arrange for some boxes and bubble wrap so we could spend the day packing in preparation for the removal company coming tonight (I am writing this at just after six o'clock – they are due at eight). As I write, we have everything packed and ready to go. Fortunately, my estimation on how many boxes would be required was accurate (a half box to spare.).

I must confess that I have been concerned about Petra's safety whilst she is visiting or that she will be present when an attack or attempt on my life occurs. With this in mind, I decided to hire a car and take her away to a nice hotel in Perthshire for the next two nights. Her flight is not until late Friday afternoon, so we have plenty of time.

I do not currently own a car as most of my time is spent in Edinburgh city centre, so I tend to walk everywhere (although I take the occasional bus or taxi if the weather turns nasty). As such, I just rent a car if and when needed. I am certainly not the best driver in the world (which I put down to lack of practice) but I am careful and I have not had an accident yet.

I just hope that does not change anytime soon.

Thursday June 30th

Friday July 1st

Saturday July 2nd

I think that my life is just getting stranger and stranger at the moment and just when I have a couple of 'normal' days something bizarre happens, but I will get to that in a moment.

Perthshire was beautiful and even the weather favoured us. We spent most of the time walking around the towns and villages and making full use of the car by driving across the region. Petra was delighted at the surprise and I actually think this may have made leaving Edinburgh slightly easier for her due to the distraction. We drove back yesterday after lunch and headed straight to the airport. Petra is not someone who tends to show her emotions but I could clearly see she was upset when it was time for us to part. I must admit that my eyes were filling up also, but I was also happy she was going back to the Czech Republic safe and unharmed from her trip here; especially after what happened today (I am getting to that part soon).

After dropping off the car, I headed over to see Alex. We checked online and there had been no further updates yet, however, Alex has been doing his own investigating in my absence. One of his 'contacts' (I dare not ask.) has established that Hugo is working for a shipping company in Australia. He has been with the same company for the last seven years and spends most of his time in Sydney. There is still no news on Leyton or anything about Sarah, but Alex is working on it. Alex and I ended up having a few too many glasses of wine so I ended up sleeping on his sofa.

After breakfast, Alex agreed to come to mine for the day. I thought that with an empty flat waiting (and a free weekend now Dad was in Spain) I might need the company. I think Alex wanted the company too and as it turned out we were both right. When we arrived at the flat, there was a package waiting for me.

You would think that under the circumstances I would have been careful, overly cautious even. I am not sure if it was the lingering hangover that was to blame, but I picked up the package and opened it without thinking. The package was small, small enough to fit through the letter box. It was a brown, padded envelope (roughly the size that would fit a hardback book) and my name and address were printed on a sticker on the front. When I opened up the envelope, I reached inside to put out the object contained within. There were no notes or letters, no additional packaging and no receipt.

It was just a plain baby's dummy.

Sunday July 3rd

Alex and I spent much of yesterday, and today, scratching our heads over my 'little gift'.

Although there were no clues linking the item to the notes (expect perhaps the complete weirdness of the situation) we are working under the assumption that they are. I called D.I. McCreedy who came over this morning to collect it. He said that there was not much to report back to me about the investigation at this time. He did state that he had sent a couple of constables to talk to my neighbours (which made me feel a little uneasy) but no one had seen anything unusual or suspicious. They were also unable to provide any information or clues about the broken door (which has now been replaced rather than mended). He also said that he has a team working through some CCTV footage of the surrounding area, however, there are not many cameras in the vicinity of my flat so it does not look too promising.

Returning to the item, Alex and I have considered the following (in no particular order) –

1 – Baby – is a child involved in all of this?
2 – Childish – is it a reference to me or my behaviour at some point?
3 – Dummy – a reference to me not working out what this situation relates to?
4 – Birth – my birth or someone else's birth or birthday?

These were our main ideas, although, we did come up with a few more.

Perversely, I actually want another note or clue.

Monday July 4th

I spent virtually all day thinking about the child's dummy (child's play?) today. I decided to do (or at least pretend to do) some more auditing as it keeps me away from Darth and the rest of the staff.

I just cannot seem to get my head round any of this. Lukas – he is not a baby so I do not think it relates to him. I was Godfather to my cousin's son, however, they live in the USA and I do not see them often, so it cannot relate to him. The dummy itself held not further clues; it was white in colour (unisex) so no further hints there.

If I thought the notes and attacks were bad enough, this is just taking it even further.

Tuesday July 5th

I received a message from Sarah's friend today.

After the usual pleasantries (nice to hear from you, I am well thanks for asking, etc.) she confirmed that she had lost contact with Sarah shortly after she moved to London. She knows that she joined a small law firm in London (Flowers and something she seems to recall) but lost contact after that. It is not much to go on, however, it is something.

Alex, as expected, is already on the case.

Wednesday July 6th

I must be going out of my head, but I am going to London next week.

I am well aware that Alex is completely off his head, however to prove the point further he is coming with me. We have a small lead and we need to follow it up. I should explain at this point that Alex has a wide network of friends and associates that he keeps in contact with. He does this for career purposes; however, this certainly suits an amateur sleuth. He contacted a good lawyer friend of his who is based in London and told him he was seeking the name of a particular law firm. His friend confirmed that the firm he was looking for was 'Even and Flowers'.

I am sure that we could have called or e-mailed them for some information, however, Alex insisted that we must follow it up on a face to face basis.

Thursday July 7th

Friday July 8th

I got too drunk with Alex last night to write anything, but today, I need to document what has happened. Hugo has been in contact.

As I guess was expected, his e-mail was not pleasant reading. He stated that he does not want me to contact him and was just replying out of courtesy. His life is fine; however, Leyton's could be better. He went downhill after I left and a year or so later he was sent to The Priory in London to beat his multiple addictions (Hugo's father is an extremely wealthy, well respected businessman, so I suspect he funded all of this). When he came out sober, he refused to return to Australia and managed to secure a job in London which allowed him to stay. He only phones home on Christmas day to wish the family well and confirm his continued sobriety.

With Leyton believed to still be in London, this is another lead for us to follow up there. As such, I decided to book my fortnight holiday starting on Monday (which is when we fly down). Alex has just finished another portrait commission, which he has described as 'anti-recession flaunting' by his unnamed client. I could tell by his description of his artwork that he is pleased with the outcome.

I also think he enjoys his own little bit of anti-recession flaunting now and again.

Saturday July 9th

Alex has once again come up trumps with his side of the investigation. He managed to get one step closer to Leyton.

To my knowledge, Alex has never taken drugs. He once told me 'Old Chap, to abuse one's precious and talented brain cells, with the insertion of chemicals, is the equivalent of urinating in the Trevi Fountain'. That said he has often found himself surrounded with drug users due to his chosen profession (and me previously for good measure). He once said that 95% of his 'artistic acquaintances' were regular users and most had visited The Priory (although he suspects that many did it for publicity rather than sobriety). One of his acquaintances just happened to meet Leyton on one of his visits.

I had calculated that Leyton must have visited within a three year period of my return to Edinburgh. This timeframe coincided with three of his acquaintances making regular visits during that time (surprisingly, perhaps, all three are currently clean and sober). One of these three, an actor, spent most of those years in and out of the clinic which meant that he knew the staff and addicts who were attending very well. He remembers a blond haired Aussie called Leyton (who had reminded him of a surfer) and recalls that his father had sent him over from Australia on account of his embarrassment to the family. He also remembers that Leyton had two goals back then, one was to get clean and the other was to stay in London. He did not wish to return to his 'embarrassed family'.

I cannot believe we managed to get so much information so quickly; however, Alex never ceases to amaze me at a time like this. He is also so driven (borderline OCD perhaps) when he has a project that interests him so maybe it should not have come as such a surprise. Knowing Alex, I hate to think how little sleep he has had this week.

With his actor friend currently 'treading the boards' in London's West End, we also found another reason for our trip.

Sunday July 10th

Our flight is at six in the morning tomorrow, so I am heading for an early night.

I have really no idea what I am doing on this trip, if truth be told, or what I hope to achieve in London. What will happen if I find Sarah or Leyton? I can hardly approach them and say to them, 'Hey, how are you doing, long time, no see. Is there any chance that you are threatening to kill me this year for some reason?'

I think the best thing to do is take a back seat role on this trip, which is what I normally do when out with Alex anyway. He seems to have more (and better) ideas than I have managed to come up with thus far. I guess it will be a case of wait and see.

I just hate to think what he has packed in his suitcase.

Monday July 11th

I am not too sure where to start today's entry, though I must state for the record that Alex is in his extreme element once again.

Today was a 'set up day'; no work was undertaken on the investigation itself. Alex arrived at the airport wearing a white summer suit, open-toed sandals and a Panama hat. He was bright and cheery (despite the early hour and his evident lack of sleep) and was looking forward to 'our little investigative adventure'.

We arrived early in London and got a taxi to Soho where Alex promised the best breakfast in London. Once we had completed our over-priced and under-portioned meal, Alex stepped outside to make a couple of phone calls. He had insisted in making arrangements for our accommodation, so we had not booked any hotels. With a wink and smile, confirming he had completed his task, we spent a couple of hours perusing the area before heading to a small café to get our daily caffeine hit. As we were finishing up, a courier headed in with a small package and was pointed by the counter staff to Alex. Duly signed for, he opened the package and removed a set of keys.

'Our humble abode for as long as we remain in London'

The 'humble abode' turned out to be a two million pound riverside penthouse. Another associate of Alex (all he let on was he was a well known television personality) is currently filming a documentary in the USA. He is happy to let us use the apartment for as long as we wished as he is not due back to the UK until October.

When we entered the apartment, it was breathtaking. I swear, I have never been so speechless in my whole life. The views across the city were outstanding and the interior design was worth the vast sums, I suspect, spent on it. There was no obvious clue to the owner's identity, and Alex was remaining tight-lipped.

After dinner we decide to unpack, with each of us having our own guest bedroom (of which there were a further two). I could not resist a look at what Alex had packed in his suitcase and I was left a little dumbfounded.

Amongst other possessions, he had packed –

- Five plain white t-shirts
- Five pairs of jeans (all plain but in different shades of blue)
- Two pairs of plain black sports trainers (unbranded)
- Five baseball hats (all different colours, however, once again plain with no logo or brand noted)
- Three styles of sunglasses, plain black without logo

He described this as his 'undercover attire' which was to be used to 'blend into the unfashionable population of the capital'. He explained that the outfit was designed so not to stand out in a crowd and the bright coloured hat would divert attention from any facial features.

And once again, I was left speechless.

Tuesday July 12th

I got up early this morning and called Petra to let her know that I was visiting London with Alex for a week or two. She was leaving the house when I called, so we did not speak long and I agreed to call her when I got back to Edinburgh. I also called Dad and he was settling well in Spain, despite the early sunburn obtained.

This afternoon we met with Alex's actor friend, 'a well known face from the wonder that is the Great British theatre the dire world of television'. I shall just refer to him as Simon.

Simon is considerably older than Alex and I; however, the two friends are obviously very fond of each other. Alex had written a play during his time at university which Simon had been passed. He contacted Alex to confirm that he wanted to direct the play and 'take it out to the masses'. It was 'a critically acclaimed, commercially disastrous venture' according to Simon. Although they do not meet very often, they have remained good friends ever since.

Alex explained to Simon that I was trying to locate Leyton to discuss some 'unfinished business' from before I had lost contact and Simon appeared happy with this vague explanation. He said that he did not keep contact with any of the other 'guests' (it was discouraged for privacy reasons) but did meet him a couple of times in the years since. The last time they met was in a West End pub about six months ago. They spoke briefly (acknowledging the matching glasses of mineral water) and Simon asked how he was 'coping on the outside'. He said that he was doing well; he had a good job doing some administration work for a small law firm and was saving to start studying part time for a law degree.

Unfortunately, Simon did not get the name of the law firm but he confirmed the name of the pub. He also remembered that it was around six o'clock in the evening (he was headed to the theatre and had to arrive there before seven o'clock for make up) and Leyton was wearing a business suit. This would indicate the pub was close to his office perhaps (might even be his regular).

Is this another clue, maybe?

Wednesday July 13th

Thursday July 14th

Friday July 15th

We decided to spend the last few days concentrating our efforts on finding Leyton, and tonight we did.

We visited the pub, The Dissident, each night from around five o'clock in the afternoon staying until eleven. We positioned ourselves at a corner table for two. I kept my back to the door and bar area, looking almost into a corner with Alex sitting directly across from me watching the crowd over my shoulder. When anyone came in with the faintest resemblance to Leyton, I would glace quickly over to confirm any suspicions to Alex. The first two nights were without luck; however, tonight we got lucky.

He arrived just after six o'clock, business suit still on, with a group of three others of similar dress. I gave Alex a nod then slipped to the toilet to try and get a better look without being noticed. As I came out from the toilet I was able to steal a proper look and, despite the passing of many years, I was in no doubt it was him.

At this point of the proceedings, my part was complete. I left Alex in the pub and headed back to the apartment. Alex is planning to do some surveillance work and try and obtain some further background.

All I can do is write this entry and await his return.

Saturday July 16th

Alex has left me to myself today and is undertaking further watching of Leyton.

Last night Alex remained in the bar, laptop to hand, pretending to work on his latest novel. The pub is a small one and quite quiet, despite its location, so he was able to blend in. He had the perfect view of Leyton and his colleagues and was close enough to listen in to parts of their conversation. From what he was able to deduct from the discussion, Leyton is well liked, hardworking and his colleagues are fully supportive of his plans to study law. They all have a dislike for their boss (who should have retired years ago and was unable to move on with the growing firm), however, they have a great passion about the business.

When Leyton chose to leave just after seven, Alex followed him from a distance. Leyton stopped at a bookshop then collected a coffee to go before heading home on the tube.

Alex had the foresight to buy an unlimited travel pass and was able to continue with his tailing. As well as keeping his laptop in his rucksack, he had a collection of hats which he chose to change a few times. Leyton got off at Clapham tube station and followed him to his flat. Although Alex did not linger long, he got the impression that he lived alone (he waited until a light went on then left).

There is a coffee shop across from Leyton's flat, so Alex is heading off there first thing this morning with his laptop, hats and a new found sense of adventure.

Sunday July 17th

Alex had a fruitless day yesterday and did not see Leyton once, so we decided to have a day off today which allowed Alex to return to wearing his 'normal' clothes.

We had a pleasant enough day, however, I was not able to enjoy it fully on the account of my worry. I thought that the trip would serve me well, getting out of Edinburgh to the safety (?) of London. I just worry that we may be heading into the Lion's Den. What if Leyton is involved? What if Alex is discovered following him? What will I do when I get back home to Edinburgh? What will be awaiting me when I get there?

Alex, on the other hand, is enjoying his stint playing private detective (he has promoted himself from amateur sleuth). 'One played a private detective on the stage once, much better in real life though Old Chap'. I think I am making a good job of masking my fear, but the thought that I may die is really starting to haunt me. In fact, death is not the frightening part for me; it is the process of dying. If I am to be murdered will it be quick, over before I know it? What if it is a revenge killing, will I be made to suffer? It got me thinking of all the worst case scenarios – torture, a pain intolerable. It takes me back to my history lessons at school, when soldiers had a poison capsule hidden in their teeth that they could use for a quick death in times of capture.

I'm not sure how easy it would be to get one in the twenty first century.

Monday July 18th

Alex set off this morning first thing in pursuit of Leyton. It is now nearly eleven o'clock, he has not returned and his phone is switched off.

I am sure that I keep hearing noises from close by, sometimes I think that they may even be coming from somewhere within the penthouse. I hate being here alone, I keep thinking of the poison capsule. Should I put myself out of my misery – just end it myself before anyone gets hurt? Please, please make Alex safe. I keep asking myself the same question, over and over.

Why did I get him involved in the first place?

Tuesday July 19th

Alex arrived back safely just after midnight. He forgot to charge his phone and, when it ran out of battery, he forgot all about it as he was too busy following Leyton all day today. If I ever thought that this trip was a waste of time, Alex has once again proved me wrong. Something he found out today took my breath away, but we shall come to that later.

Alex arrived for breakfast early at the coffee shop across from Leyton's flat. He sat at a window seat but facing away from the flats main door. Alex has a metallic Zippo lighter (despite not smoking – purely for show) and sat this on the table using the reflection as a mirror to keep sight of the door. After finishing his toast he saw Leyton leaving the flat.

Leyton then came into the shop to order a coffee to go and Alex walked to the counter to settle his bill as Leyton was departing. He managed to leave the shop in time to start another tail and was able to follow Leyton on the tube back to his office.

After entering through the main door of the office block, Leyton entered his office to go about his working day. Alex went for a stroll around the area (to prevent any suspicion, though in a city as busy as London I am not sure he would be noticed) before returning back to the main door of the office block. Alex took a note of all the businesses based there, although there was one in particular that caught his attention.

Alex headed to various cafes (anxious once again to prevent suspicion) to do some further research on the business that took his notice. At five o'clock, he headed back to the office to wait for Leyton's exit. He watched the various staff members leave and one in particular, a woman, seemed to be acting a little suspicious. Leyton left not long after the woman and started to walk in a similar direction. After a good ten to twenty minutes, Leyton arrived at a restaurant where he was greeted by the woman from his office block. The restaurant was far enough away from the office to suggest that they were keen to meet in a location where they would not be noticed. Alex remained in the area awaiting the couple's exit, before following them both. He noticed that Leyton was being more aware of his surroundings and being more vigilant so he had to be very careful not to be noticed, however, he was confident that his presence was not observed.

The couple walked further away still from the office and headed into a pub for drinks and some time together. At this point it became clear that they were in a relationship, but not one that they wanted other people to know about. It may be just an office affair at an early stage, or it could be an extra marital affair. The relationship, however, was not the information that took my breath away. It was the name of the business that Alex believes Leyton works for with the mystery girl.

The name on the door, amongst others, was Even and Flowers.

Wednesday July 20th

Thursday July 21st

Yesterday, and on Tuesday, Alex spent time around the offices of Even and Flowers continuing his watch and research. I am due back to work on Monday, so we need to leave on Sunday. Alex has agreed to come back with me despite his perverse enjoyment of playing detective. We have the flights booked now, however, we are determined not to leave until we know if the mystery woman is, or is connected with, Sarah.

The slight advantage is that the two people we are looking for are connected to Even and Flowers, though that has maybe added more questions rather than providing any answers. Our plan today and tomorrow is to monitor the offices together and do some further digging. Alex has a few plans in that regard, so once again I will allow him to lead the way. We are possibly taking a risk today that I may be recognised, however, I have dressed similarly to Alex with that in mind (black t-shirt rather that white though).

We have just finished getting ready and Alex is currently staring at me tapping his watch.

I guess it is time to go.

Friday July 22nd

The mystery woman was not Sarah and, despite Alex's best efforts, no one has heard from her.

Yesterday we spent time around the offices as planned and the woman did not come out until after six o'clock. She met with, and embraced, a man outside the office and then headed off to a nearby restaurant. We decided to remain in that vicinity for our own curiosity and were able to establish that the couple were wearing matching wedding rings. At least that is one mystery solved.

Today we decided to move our focus and efforts on to Sarah. We both agreed we had as much information that we were likely to get on Leyton for now. For what Alex witnessed and found out, he cannot see a reason why Leyton would be responsible. He appears to be just trying to get his life back together and seems to be on the right track. It is hard to disagree with this theory, but I just have a niggling doubt mainly because I was responsible for his downfall in the first place.

We have not been as successful getting information about Sarah, but Alex did find out something very interesting. Before I get to that, I must document what Alex did next.

After making some calls, and failing to get very far, Alex decided to take matters into his own hands. Posing as an Edinburgh lawyer, he made an appointment to meet with Mr Flowers. He was able to transfer his summer suit into business dress quite convincingly and arrived for the appointment. He told Mr Flowers that he was acting (very clever Alex) on behalf of a distant relative of Sarah who needed to track her down. To Alex's estimation, Mr Flowers was in his early seventies. He appeared like someone that was keen to hold on to his past glories, horrified with the idea of retiring and happy to be of any service he could be.

Alex was in the meeting for a good couple of hours and had to listen to a lot of reminiscing before he got back to the subject of Sarah. He was not able to offer much information as Sarah had left many years before. He remembers her well and he recalls she was a hard worker and was a great loss to the firm when she left. Sarah did not remain in contact with him or any other members of the staff as far as he was aware. It seemed that Alex was heading for a dead end until Alex asked him if he had a note of her last known address. Mr Flowers confirmed he had, 'I always keep a record of my staff, almost like a diary of past events nowadays' and was happy to pass it on to a fellow man of the trade. When Alex told me the address, I could not believe my ears.

She was, or had been, living in Clapham.

Saturday July 23rd

Answers –

- Leyton is alive and well in London
- Leyton is trying to get his life on track
- Sarah has not been traced, no longer living at the Clapham address

Questions –

- Do Leyton and Sarah know each other?
- Is Leyton studying law for his future or for an ulterior motive?
- Why the connection with Even and Flowers?
- Why the connection with Clapham?
- Is this just a co-incidence?
- Would someone study law whilst breaking the law?
- Why did Sarah leave Even and Flowers?
- Where is Sarah?

Yes, definitely more questions than answers.

Sunday July 24th

I am back in Edinburgh.

I do not feel safe.

I feel vulnerable.

I hate being on my own again.

I am frightened of every noise I hear outside.

I feel sick.

I do not want to go to work tomorrow, or ever again.

I do not want to die.

Monday July 25th

I realise that I am at my worst when I am alone. I was fine in London with Alex, except the days I was in the apartment alone. Even so, I knew then I was relatively safe. Alex and I got back from London at lunchtime, so I had all day in the flat (hence my ramblings in yesterday's entry).

Work was a good distraction as it gave me something to focus on. I stayed until well after eight o'clock as I felt I needed to keep myself busy (even Sue left before me, albeit by about ten minutes). I think I will have to think of things to do to take up more of my time. Many of the people closest to me are now gone, Dad, Petra, Wills, Mike.

I arrived home late having headed to a restaurant to eat a meal (trying to kill more time). I had a message to call D.I. McCreedy; however, I will leave that until tomorrow. I wonder if he has any further news for me.

I expect disappointment once again though.

Tuesday July 26th

I called D.I. McCreedy from work and, although the police do not appear to be any closer to finding the culprit, he was able to confirm an interesting development on the investigation. He has been able to secure the services of Lars on my case and another couple of cases he is also working on.

I called Lars when I got home and he confirmed that he has the opportunity of promotion within Lothian and Borders police and has been offered a secondment into the new role. Lars has fully trained another forensic officer in Strathclyde police and she is 'exceptional' and is more than capable of filling his shoes, therefore, she is seconded into Lars' current role at the same time.

He confirmed that his first task was looking at the package and dummy. There was once again little to go on, though he was able to confirm that it was definitely linked to the notes (something to do with ink samples). The perpetrator is very careful not to leave any trace or evidence. The package had a number of finger prints; however, these would include mine, the postman's, letter handler, etc. so little use. He expects that the sender used gloves as they had done when the notes were sent. The one thing Lars did notice was some small dimples or indents on the address label which indicated that the sender used tweezers when labelling the package (and once again he commented that they were very, very good).

I just hope that Lars proves to be better.

Wednesday July 27th

Thursday July 28th

Friday July 29th

I am going out for drinks with Alex tonight, another welcome diversion.

I have spent most of the last few days in work, finishing late, eating in the safety of a busy restaurant before getting a taxi home.

I just do not want to take any undue risks.

I have to get to the end of this.

Saturday July 30th

Last night was very, very good and Alex and I got exceptionally drunk.

I managed to convince him to stay at mine and admitted my vulnerability to him. I am scared that I am putting him at risk, however, he would not hear of it. 'You know I will always be the perfect chaperone to ensure you come to no harm Old Boy'. I am also welcome to stay at his any time, but I do not wish to take advantage of his support and kindness. He is confident that we shall get to the bottom of this one way or another.

I just wish I could share his optimism.

Sunday July 31st

Monday August 1st

Another package came today. It arrived in the post before I was due to leave for work, so I phoned in sick (which physically, I had just been).

I called Lars first and as it transpires he was on a train to Edinburgh heading for his first official day in his new role (since the appointment, he had been working from his lab in Glasgow). He made a phone call to make some re-arrangements then called me back to confirm he would come straight to my flat from the station. He arrived just after ten o'clock and got his equipment ready. I did not touch anything; I knew straight away what it was.

Lars got to work straight away, he had much of what he needed his with him in his portable case ('I never leave my good stuff lying around; you would not believe the amount of thieves in the forensic department.'). I stayed far enough away so as not to disturb him, but close enough to observe what he was doing. He spent what felt an age on the package's envelope, confirming it was the same as before. Again it had been posted from Edinburgh and finger prints would be useless. He was unable to confirm any obvious trace evidence but needed to take it to the lab to be fully satisfied. I held my breath as he started to open the package and slowly remove the contents.

It took me a little while to work out what is was exactly. Lars remained quiet throughout, meticulously focusing in his work. And then, after what had felt like a lifetime, I saw exactly what the object inside was.

It was a small model of a coffin.

Tuesday August 2nd

Lars came over today to collect my little 'gift'. I think it made little sense to him either; however, he collected the item in an evidence bag (which he had to collect this morning) and headed off to his lab. In work mode, Lars gives very little away – he is the ultimate professional.

D.I. McCreedy called this evening to confirm that there was little in the way of an update on the case (or getting to the bottom of it).

I have not eaten since breakfast yesterday (which I in turned flushed down the toilet when it came back up again). My stomach just will not settle at the moment, but I need to try and get into work tomorrow.

I wonder if my good friend Darth is still talking to me.

Wednesday August 3rd

I received interesting information at work today from Claire.

Darth was fine this morning and asked how I was feeling. I confirmed that I was not feeling great; however, I was able to cope with a day in the office. I ate some toast mid morning, which has stayed down, but nothing since. I just do not have the appetite.

Anyway, back to the information from Claire. One thing I must state for the record is that I detest (and always have detested) office gossip. I believe that we should just get on with our work and our colleagues. As such, I rarely get to hear anything that goes on. Today, however, I was party to some information that confused me and intrigued me in equal measures.

Claire met me at the coffee machine (I sense that this was on purpose rather than by accident). She asked if I was aware that I had a secret admirer. Of course, I told her that I had no idea of this. She then told me that someone had been round, whilst I was off, asking lots of questions about me, my family, my love life, etc. I do not talk much about these sorts of things in the office, so I am not sure what information was shared.

In normal circumstances, I would not have taken the conversation any further. These, however, are not normal circumstances. If someone was taking an interest in me, it could be a clue. Claire, I guess, sensed that I was keen to find out who this person was and was clearly enjoying the power she held over me, drip feeding me morsels of information. Like a spoiled schoolgirl, she asked me to guess who it was. I managed to retain my composure, despite my heart beating a little faster than normal, as I did not want my feelings to surface. I did not have to retain this composure for long as, much to Claire's surprise and disappointment, I guessed correct first time.

It had been Sue.

Thursday August 4th

Friday August 5th

Saturday August 6th

Friday night plus Alex plus drinks equals one night of freedom.

Well not quite but I needed the company and the alcohol in equal measures. I spent most of today in bed recovering (and trying to remember everything we talked about last night).

I have still been mostly avoiding food, a few slices of toast and glasses of orange juice being the main diet for the last few days. As such, the alcohol kicked in quickly and I was made to suffer the consequences this morning. I do not remember getting into the taxi last night, just getting out (on my own) and trying to navigate my key into its lock.

Alex and I spent most of the evening (as far as I remember it) discussing the coffin and Sue. Starting with the coffin, its obvious symbolisation is death. It could, however, also relate to something buried (an item, a memory, a body?). It could also be a play on works coffin/coughing (Alex came up with this idea) and relate to smoking drugs. The Sue situation is equally puzzling. Why is she asking questions about me? Is she trying to get some background to help her career, or hinder mine? Is she involved in the threats? Is she just interested in me?

Once again I find my brain full of questions and desperately seeking answers.

Sunday August 7th

Alex came over again today and I was glad of the company (mainly due to my insecurity and for the sake of my sanity).

I decided that, given how serious things had escalated in recent months, I should make plans should anything happen to me. Alex was not keen to hear this, though I insisted that it be discussed if only to put one small issue out of my mind. I have already made certain arrangements with my solicitor including a fresh will which will see the bulk of my estate go to Alex and my other friends.

Alex already has keys to my flat (although he will only use these in emergency situations – his choice) and access to the safe I keep this diary in. I also have a separate notebook kept in there which I have made notes and ideas about the threats. In recent weeks, I have been adding notes and updates to my autobiography and have kept a copy of this in the safe also. If

I am killed, Alex is to empty the contents of the safe and retain them. He has to use the contents to the best of his ability, to find my killer, but should not trust anyone. If I am killed in my flat, and he is first to find me, I have left a prepaid envelope (addressed to Alex) in there also which he should place all the items in and place in the post box outside the flat before calling the police.

As I was telling this to Alex, he was shaking his head and telling me that this was pointless and nothing was going to happen to me. I assume he was saying this to try and reassure me, and before I may have agreed with him.

Now, however, I am not so sure.

Monday August 8th

I went into work and saw Sue for the first time since Claire told me about her asking questions about me. Sue had been on a course since last Wednesday, so I had not seen her. I tried to make a conscious effort to avoid her (without appearing that I was avoiding her) and not make any signs that I knew that she was asking about me. I was successful for most of the day, though, she came to see me late afternoon with some issues that she wanted to run past me.

It may have been paranoia setting in once more, but I know she already knew how to deal with these issues. She may, of course, have just been seeking some reassurance and there was nothing untoward in it.

That stated, I think it is time that Alex and I try to find out some more about Sue.

Tuesday August 9th

I received a call from Petra tonight, although it was not a call I was expecting. It appears our relationship is now over.

Since she moved back to the Czech Republic I have not been calling her as often as I should have. We had a nice time in Perthshire when she last came over and, looking back, I felt relaxed being out of Edinburgh. I think, however, that my focus was far from one hundred per cent on Petra and this may have shown. The few phone calls I did make were short and I found that I did not have much to say. My mind has been so occupied with everything that has been going on that there was not much for me to discuss. And the one thing on my mind, I did not want to share with her.

Petra said that she knew that things were not going to work out when she was flying back to the Czech Republic. Not long after her return, she met an old boyfriend from school. Petra assured me that nothing has happened yet, but they have rekindled their friendship and I suspect that they both want to pursue this further.

I remained mostly silent as Petra told me all of this, as different emotions ran through me. Petra is a very special person and maybe she was the right person at the wrong time for me. I suspect that possibly I was the wrong person and the right time for her. She said that she would never forget me, that I was the first person she had had a relationship with since her husband died and, for that, I would be forever in her heart. With all the feelings I was having at this time, the overriding feeling was one of relief.

Despite my hurt, I could not help feeling that Petra and her family would now be truly safe.

Wednesday August 10th

Someone is following me.

I can sense it.

I can feel it.

I just can not see it.

Thursday August 11th

The worst time of day is night time. If I leave work at a reasonable hour (for example, before seven o'clock in the evening) then it is still light and I walk home relatively relaxed. The problem is that I have to spend more hours, on my own, in the flat until I wake up in the morning to head off for work. If I stay at work late, the walk home is dark and I feel more vulnerable. In these occasions, I sometimes take a taxi or walk in a more vigilant manner.

Such an occasion happened last night. The city is busy (the festival is currently in full throw) and I feel more exposed in a crowd. If someone wanted to kill me, then a crowded street watching a performing artist would be a perfect opportunity. Everyone's attention is focused elsewhere and they could do it quickly in passing before disappearing into the crowd. So last night walking home, I found myself looking all around and in all directions. I saw many faces, some alone, some in couples and some in groups. Many of these faces appeared to be looking at me. Could it be one of these people? Would someone in a group be responsible and hold a secret plot of revenge that they have kept close to themselves?

I found myself walking on the road when ever possible, avoiding busy pavements and darkened corners (of which there are many in the centre of Edinburgh, especially in the Old Town where the festival is at its busiest). For every hazard I pass on my way home, there quickly appears another one. My walk home should only take around ten minutes, however, it currently feels like hours.

And I feel like I am being watched on my every step home.

Friday August 12th

Alex insists that we attend a show tonight.

He has an old friend making her directorial debut at one of the bigger theatres in Edinburgh. Alex believes that this is fully justified and his friend is 'of remarkably, exceptional talent'. His friend, however, is not so sure and is having opening night nerves.

She is currently of a nervous disposition? I know how she feels.

Saturday August 13th

NEVER AGAIN (again.)

It is eight o'clock in the evening and I am still struggling to open my eyes. I am mostly a beer drinker and spirits are only taken in moderation and on special occasions. I think that last night I may have broken every drinking rule that exists. I mixed my grapes, finished each pint with a shot, had a glass (or three) of Champagne (Alex's insistence in celebration of his friends triumphant opening night) and finished (I think) with cocktails.

Again, I do not remember much about getting home, but when I awoke (fully dressed lying on my bed under my duvet), I found Alex passed out on my sofa (wearing a Mexican Sombrero that I cannot recall seeing at all last night). When he eventually awoke, he was certainly brighter than I was and he left for home an hour or so ago. He wanted to make plans about the next stage of our investigation, but I could neither concentrate or focus on anything other than the little Death Metal band which is playing inside my skull (with guitars turned up to eleven.)

Oh God, there goes my phone, I need to stop writing now.

Sunday August 14th

I am feeling much better today after an unscheduled long lie this morning.

I did not surface until a few minutes before noon having slept right through the night last night for the first time in months. Despite the return of my focus and energies, I decided to laze around the flat, albeit, I gave it a much needed clean throughout.

The phone call last night was from Will. He has a week off from training and is coming back today; he is spending today with his family, but wants to catch up with Alex, Linda and me.

I just hope Wills is still off the alcohol – it is just too soon for me.

Monday August 15th

Tuesday August 16th

I went out with Wills, Alex and Linda last night and had a great time. I arranged a day off today so I could go out and really enjoy myself, which I certainly did.

Wills arranged to meet me at the office after work and we had a drink together alone before Alex and Linda joined us. Wills is looking great and he told me he is really enjoying his training and is determined to give his all to his police career. He realises that he spent far too many years messing around, but he has now found his focus in life. He has also been in touch with D.I. McCreedy who has been giving good career advice, having reached the rank of Inspector much sooner in his career than most.

D.I. McCreedy did not discuss my case with Wills, so I brought him up to date with the threats and the arrival of my 'little gifts'. Wills, in turn, told me that he had spoken to Mike a few times. Before he left for London, Mike had called Wills to confess all. Wills has always been the most diplomatic of the group and never one to take sides, so I suspect he was a good sounding board for Mike. Wills said that Mike has been focusing on his career and is very regretful for everything that has happened. Apparently, things are going well for him in London and he has no plans to return to Edinburgh in the foreseeable future.

When Alex and Linda arrived, we lightened the mood. Wills stayed on the soft drinks, Linda had a few glasses of wine, Alex had a couple of cocktails and I stuck with Jack Daniels and diet coke. I cannot remember how many I had, but I think it was a few more than I should have. I recall at my turn at the bar I was ordering myself doubles. I guess I was more recovered (from the other night) than I had expected.

Linda was in a good mood also and is doing well at work and in life. After a couple of glasses of wine, she let me know that she had met someone on the internet and they were having a date on Friday. She would not tell me anything about him, but she had spoken to him on the phone and he 'sounded particularly lovely'.

Linda also made a strange remark towards me. She asked why I was mixing my drink with diet coke as I looked like I should be putting on some extra pounds. Upon reflection, I must admit that I have lost some weight in recent weeks (my appetite is still AWOL), but I did not really notice. I have not weighed myself for quite a while, so it certainly was not something I had noticed. I have, however, started using a different notch on my trousers belt.

Maybe this is something else I need to watch out for?

Wednesday August 17th

Sue is still acting strange.

Darth is in London this week and Sue keeps asking me things.

I can feel Claire and the other team members watching us. I am sure we are the subject of coffee machine gossip.

I just cannot figure what on earth she is up to.

Thursday August 18th

I phoned Alex tonight and he is coming over this weekend. I think it is time that we started the next stage of our own investigation. I happen to think that it may start with Sue.

Wills and I are going out tonight as he is heading out with his family tomorrow and is going back to Police College on Saturday.

I wonder what the evening will bring.

Friday August 19th

I was not in good form at work today.

I arrived late (the first time since I started with the company), albeit only by thirty minutes. Darth is in London again today, so that was a small blessing.

Having slept in, I rushed out of the flat without breakfast (not an unusual occurrence) and without the chance to brush my teeth. Despite getting a strong coffee on arrival, I realised that I must still smell from the copious amount of Mr Daniel's finest that I consumed last night. I went out at lunch time to buy some mouthwash to bring back to the office. When I went into the Gents, I washed my face with cold water and looked up to the mirror. I was more than a little shocked at the reflection staring at me, my eyes were black and sagging, almost like a modern day Alice Cooper. My hair was all over the place and in desperate need of a trim.

I was not much use this afternoon either, when Sue came round to see me. I managed to make my excuses and did not spend much time with her, much to the obvious disappointment of the OG's (Office Gossips).

Wills was in good spirits last night, despite his lack of alcohol consumption. I, as you will have already worked out, was devoured by altogether different spirits. I have only realised this week how much I miss his company and sense of humour. I am delighted that he is happy and so passionate about his new life right now.

And upon reflection, I think it is that kind of passion that is missing in my life at this time.

Saturday August 20th

Right Steve, you need to get a couple of things sorted.

Firstly, I need to cut down on the drinking. I had not taken notice of the amount of drinking I have been doing of late until I decided to read back through the last few weeks of this diary. Secondly, I need to try and eat more regardless of my continual lack of appetite.

To help me on my way with these realisations, I undertook two tasks this morning before Alex arrived. I decided to get up early and go out for a run. It has been a while since I was last out for a run and I started to feel it early. I barely lasted twenty minutes before I started to struggle. I came home, had a shower and then headed out to purchase a set of scales to monitor my weight. I am five foot and eleven inches tall so; according to the internet site I found on my return, I should weigh one hundred and forty eight pounds. I am, what they refer to as, medium build so this should be quite accurate, although, it should fall within a range of one hundred and thirty six pounds to one hundred and seventy nine pounds (big range.).

My first weigh-in had me at exactly ten stones (or one hundred and forty pounds), so I am a little under ideal weight but well within the correct range. I honestly cannot remember the last time I weighed myself, however, I always considered myself to be around eleven stones (or one hundred and fifty four pounds). As such, I need to get somewhere inbetween.

Alex arrived just after lunch and has purchased some new 'toys'. I think Alex fancies himself as some James Bond type character. He opened his satchel (it is Alex I am talking about.) and he has bought the following items –

1 – A new laptop computer with no traceable personal information (no, I do not get it either).
2 – A listening device ('probably illegal Old Chap, but what the hell')

3 – A small mirror with an extendable handle ('for when one is trapped in a hiding corner and needs to view in all directions')
4 – Night Vision Binoculars (I really am not joking.)

Having enjoyed the experience so much in London, Alex has decided to follow Sue. He suggested that I try and become friends with her at work. I guess I already have a good working relationship with her. She is a few years younger than me, very good at her job, but apart from that I do not know much else. I am slightly worried what the OG's will make of this, so I need to proceed with caution. Alex also suggested that I try to 'friend' her on Facebook, as this would give a good insight to her personal life and her interests. I still do not really know what I am doing with this, however, I am happy to run with the idea. I feel more comfortable about befriending her in real life before I tackle Facebook.

After eating some dinner (which Alex prepared and I was able to eat and enjoy with little effort), I suddenly realised that I still have a copy of Sue's original application form from when she first joined the company. I am certain that the form also has a copy of her C.V. attached. As Alex said when I told him this –

'And that is an exceptionally, wonderful place to begin the latest stage of our exquisite adventure, Old Boy'.

Sunday August 21st

Alex and I did not do much today in relation to the investigation, except for a little further background work.

We had a further discussion regarding the autobiography, including some of my updated notes, to see if we could find any further suspects (which we could not). It got us back to talking about the three original names that came up during my initial writing. Could it really be Chris Jackson and his contact was just a front to put us off the scent? What about Leyton Ronson, is he really back on track with his life or is he after some kind of revenge? And what about Sarah James, where is she and does she fit in with this at all?

The above discussion did not get us very far and it just brought us back to Sue. Alex did manage to track her down on Facebook, but I need to approach her at work first (I do not want to go down as some kind of weird Cyber Stalker). I was trying to remember back to when Sue first started at the office. She appeared very focused on the job, right from the first day, and intent on getting a good grip on the role and its responsibilities. She did not seem to take much notice or talk much to me at the start. Is this because I was her boss at the time? Why is she taking more notice of me now? Is she interested in me for a personal relationship? Is she interested in me because she needs help with her new role? Was she promoted too quickly and now she is struggling to cope?

Once again, question after question after question.

Monday August 22nd

Tuesday August 23rd

Wednesday August 24th

Although I am still not eating as much as I should, I feel and look a lot better now.

I went and got a haircut and tidied myself up a bit before work this week. I must state, for the record, that I do take pride in my appearance and I do make an effort every day. The 'Unfortunate Friday' (as I refer to it) was a mere escalation of my not eating and drinking too much. I was fine on the other days I was in work, so it remains very much a one off. I say this, as I wondered upon reflection if Sue is attracted to me despite the bad day I had. It may be so, as she was taking an interest before this event.

Anyway, I started to engage more with Sue this week and it seems to be working in my favour. She asked me on Monday for some help with a project that Darth has asked her to do (Darth suggested that she come to me) so we went to the canteen for a coffee together to discuss it. Fortunately it is a quite in depth project, so I suggested that we meet for an hour each day to discuss progress and any issues. This, in turn, seems to have satisfied the OG's.

Today we started discussing each others life outside work. I did not let on much, mostly about my Dad moving to Spain with his new partner (I thought this was pretty safe ground to reveal). She, in turn, told me that she split up with her long term boyfriend just before she joined the company and that she was too busy to start another relationship with anyone at this time.

If truth be told I have always quite liked Sue, certainly she is one of the best workers in the office. She is completely focused and career driven, but she does not appear to get on anyone's wrong side on her way up the career ladder. She also avoids office gossip at all costs (so she told me).

We ended the conversation talking about Facebook of all things. I told her that I was a complete novice but recently joined it out of curiosity more that anything, albeit, I still do not really know what I am doing. She gave me a wink as she left the canteen saying that she would have to look me up.

When I came home, I could only face a bowl of cereal for dinner (which is starting to become a regular occurrence). I decided to log on to my e-mails only to discover that I had a 'friend request' from Sue. I immediately called Alex to let him know and ask what he thought. He is planning to start his 'observational work' on Friday and his reply was frank and straight to the point.

'Accept at once Old Boy, and then let the fun and games begin'

Thursday August 25th

Friday August 26th

Alex followed Sue from the office tonight to interesting results.

I called Alex at five o'clock from my desk to confirm that I was about to leave and that Sue was still in the office. When I left, I noticed Alex standing across the street in his non-descript outfit and red baseball hat. Had I not known that he was going to be there, or what he was wearing today, I would never have noticed him.

I headed back to my flat, only stopping for a coffee at what was once Petra's place of employment (her replacement does not make half as good a coffee as she did.). I reached the flat and entered, awaiting Alex's arrival.

Alex arrived around an hour later looking both flushed and excited. He had let himself in with the keys I had given him (this is the first time he has done this, as he always rings the intercom if he knows I am in) and ran up the flights of stairs (hence the flushed appearance – not one for much exercise is Our Alex.). Alex, with his unmistakeable grin of triumph, told me that Sue left shortly after I did and then started to follow me from a distance.

Now, I can tell you, this was a little more than unsettling on my behalf. I was trying to get close to this girl and she is now following me (I know – pot calling the kettle black.). It makes me wonder if she has been following me for a while or did she just start this evening?

Alex also commented on the fact that she was very good at tailing me (he is obviously a complete expert now). She acted very natural and no one (but himself) would have any idea what she was up to. Even when I stopped for coffee, she walked into the shop across the street, looking at items near the entrance until I had left. She continued to follow me until I reached my flat. At that point, she waited around for ten minutes watching all around (Alex was worried he was going to be spotted, however, he maintained his cover). Alex then followed her until she got on a bus which was headed south of the city (assuming that she was heading home at this point). By the way Alex spoke of Sue; I think he has competition for Rookie Spy of the Year.

I just hope that he was not spotted by Sue.

Saturday August 27th

I weighed myself today.

I now weigh one hundred and thirty eight pounds, which is two pounds less than last week.

Still within the correct range though, so I think I will head to the pub for some lunch.

Sunday August 28th

Alex and I spent today trying to work out what was Sue's agenda and what we should do next.

We started by discussing the AB3 (autobiography three) and agreed that we should try and take these further. With Chris, I thought I could try and meet him face to face which would give me a better feeling if he is genuine or not. I thought that I could make an excuse for being in the area and could e-mail him asking to meet for a drink or coffee. Strangely, I really like this idea and Alex is all for it (I think he plans to come along also, although I am not sure on what capacity). With

Leyton, Alex told me he already has a plan to take this to the next step, but he has to make some arrangements first. As for Sarah, well we just need to find her. Alex thinks if we get close to Leyton, we may find out more about the elusive Sarah.

We agreed that we cannot do much more about Sue until Alex has undertaken further observations. One possible option in the future is for me to ask her out for a drink.

I am a little apprehensive of both asking her and what her answer may be.

Monday August 29th

Tuesday August 30th

Wednesday August 31st

Thursday September 1st

I came home from work today to find a note from the post office saying that a package had been left with a neighbour. Of course, I knew at once what it was so it was with great nervousness that I knocked on the door of the flat across the landing.

Mrs Dunbar must be in her seventies and lives alone (with the exception of her cat 'Candles'). I have said hello to her a few times, however, I don't know her that well like most of my neighbours. I apologised to Mrs Dunbar, however, she said it was no trouble at all. She had the package behind her front door and said she hoped it was something nice. I smiled and retreated back to my flat to call Lars.

Lars was standing at Waverley Station awaiting his train back to Glasgow when I called. He abandoned his planned journey home and came over to my flat. He asked if he could stay overnight and I was happy to oblige. I ordered some pizzas which were delivered just after he arrived around eight o'clock. I decided to wash down my dinner with a few beers, however, Lars stuck to soft drinks as he was about to go into his 'work zone'.

The package was bigger than the others (which had fitted through my letter box) and was roughly the size of a shoe box. I noticed that it had the same label as the ones before. Lars again stated that the fingerprints on the outside were useless so he went straight to opening the package. He slowly removed a box that was contained within the packaging. I once again stood frozen on the spot awaiting the reveal. Lars seemed to take an age to open the package, but I realised he was just doing his job properly, professionally and for my benefit. I could not take my eyes off Lars' hands as he felt inside the box. Once again there was no note or other clue contained within except the item itself. Lars removed the item with great care and it took me a while to realise exactly what it was.

It was a small set of weighing scales.

Friday September 2nd

Lars was up early and thanked me for my hospitality. He was taking advantage of the stay in Edinburgh to get in early to the lab today. He told me he would be carrying out more tests and he would let me know if anything came up.

I went into work in a state of concern. I feel that I am going round in circles. The police do not have anything to go on (as far as I can see). I have some people that I suspect, but they are not obviously involved and I do not know if I could even refer to them as 'suspects'.

I guess my demeanour was spotted by Sue as she was being incredibly kind to me today. If this is an act on her part, she does it very well. Of the people I think may wish to cause me harm, Sue is the one I most hope is not involved.

Alex has been busy this week, so he has not been undertaking any further 'observations'. I called him this evening to discuss the package and he is coming over tomorrow to find out more.

He told me that his latest plan is taking shape nicely.

Saturday September 3rd

Now getting back to the scales, I guess I should explain these further and what they look like.

Firstly, they are gold in colour. They are the traditional style of weighing scales with cups on either side (the type that you place a set weight on one side and balance this with the desired amount of material on the other side).

I have a few theories about this latest object. My main thought is drug related. This type of instrument is often used in movies which allow the dealer to give out the correct 'dosage' to the user. My own drug addiction remains the lowest point of my life and I cannot help but think that this is related in some way.

Another theory could be my weight. If this is the case, then the perpetrator must be close enough to witness my recent weight loss. Given the contents of the previous notes, this is certainly viable.

Alex came over and added his own theory, which is related to balance. His theory is based on the type of scales used being operated under the physics of balance. This has numerous possibilities in itself. It could relate to life/death, weak/strong, using/clean, drunk/sober, the list is endless. It could also relate to being unbalanced which my life and mind certainly are both at present.

Alex is staying over tonight. He says he has one final phone call to make tomorrow and then his planning will be over. I have been informed that I 'will be stunned to the core of my soul at the sheer genius of this master plan'.

I hold my breath…

Sunday September 4th

Stunned to the core of my soul I certainly am.

I really have no idea how he does these things, but he has arranged for another of his acquaintances to go and work in the offices of Even and Flowers for a fortnights work experience. The person in question is an up and coming actor who had been working as a stand in actor for the last ten years in London's West End; however, he has been mainly unused and feels let down by the whole experience. A few years ago, he decided to begin a law degree course with the Open University whilst trying to make it as a successful actor.

Alex called Mr Flowers (under his previous pseudonym) and asked if he could possibly do him this favour for a dear friend. Of course, old Mr Flowers was delighted to oblige and is currently finalising the arrangements. He is looking to confirm a start date of Monday the twelfth of September which is ideal as the actor has a small part starting at the beginning of October.

Alex's acquaintance is a friend from his school days who he trusts wholly and unreservedly. All his friend knows is that he has to gather information on Leyton who is currently working there and Sarah who used to work there. The level of trust allows for no questions asked. In return, Alex has arranged a good part in a big play due to start next year as well as gaining some good experience for his law degree.

I am not sure if this is getting more exciting or more ridiculous.

Monday September 5th

Sue is on holiday this week.

It seems strange to think of it now, however, I cannot recall her being off much this year. It makes me wonder if she has taken time off whilst I was also off. It could be that she has deliberately not taken the time given the new job and promotion in quick succession. With all the holidays mounting up she may be forced into taking some holidays, hence her absence from work this week.

I found the application form with the C.V. attached and took it over to Alex's flat after work. Alex made dinner (something with venison, although I have no idea what.) and we studied the C.V. afterwards. The first interesting point we noted was that there is no obvious link to London. The whole Leyton/Sarah connection is still playing heavily on my mind. She grew up just outside Glasgow and was educated at Strathclyde University in Glasgow where she left with a degree in Business Studies. After her graduation, she worked in a Building Society for a number of years on a Management Trainee programme; however, she was made redundant when it was taken over by a bank. She moved to Edinburgh shortly after, taking on a number of temporary positions until she applied to her current employer. The application also shows that she lives on Leith Walk.

Of course, this final piece of information was of great interest to Alex, who took a note of the address. I turned a blind eye at this point, before putting the application back into my brief case.

I shall return the application to the office first thing tomorrow morning.

Tuesday September 6th

I weighed myself again today.

I had planned to weigh myself every Saturday, however, after everything that has happened in the last week I had forgotten all about it.

I currently weigh one hundred and thirty four pounds, another four pounds less than the last time.

Wednesday September 7th

Thursday September 8th

Alex called.

Sue is still living in her flat on Leith Walk. Apparently today she went to the laundrette, the Post Office and to the supermarket.

It is hardly the typical day of a Psycho Killer now, qu'est-ce que c'est?

Friday September 9th

I am meeting Chris on Sunday.

I was doing some research online during the night last night and discovered that one of my favourite Scottish singer/songwriters is playing a concert tomorrow night in Manchester. I called Alex and I ended up booking two tickets for the concert, two flights to Manchester and a hotel room (no chance of me doing this alone now).

I e-mailed Chris to say that I am around on Sunday as the flight back is not until the evening. Chris e-mailed back to confirm that he was free and we are meeting in the city centre for drinks.

Eye to eye, I am confident that I will be able to confirm if he is being truthful or not.

Saturday September 10th

Sunday September 11th

I have just arrived back from the airport having spent the weekend in Manchester (I decided to leave the diary in the safe whist I was away.

I have never been to Manchester before and I certainly was not there for a tourist visit this time, so do not expect any commentary to this effect. Alex and I arrived mid afternoon, found our hotel, checked in and headed out for dinner before the concert. I did manage to enjoy the concert despite my mind focusing on my meeting with Chris today. I had a number of beers over dinner and at the concert to help me relax, but it did not really work.

I woke up early this morning and drank gallons of orange juice at breakfast to clear my head. Although I was meeting Chris for drinks, I had to ensure I was completely focused, so I decided to stay clear of alcohol.

We met outside the bar at three o'clock and I recognised Chris straight away. He had put on some weight since I last saw him; however, it seemed to suit him. He greeted me with a warm handshake and an even warmer smile. At once I found myself relax in his company in spite of the feeling of reservations I had within.

We entered the bar, which was Chris' favourite in Manchester, and he was greeted by the barman (who was obviously a friend). Chris made a great fuss over his 'good, good friend from school', 'been too long', 'missed him much', etc. I noticed Alex sitting at the end of the bar, sipping a cocktail under his beloved Trilby. Chris insisted on buying the drinks, only for the barman (who turned out to be the owner) insisting that they were on the house. I made excuses about driving later to avoid drinking and settled on a fresh orange juice and lemonade. Chris had a pint of some type of local ale.

We stayed at the bar chatting about the old days at school and the things we used to get up to. The conversation ultimately headed towards the fall out as we both apologised profusely before agreeing that we were both just 'daft lads' at the time. I noticed Alex smile at this point which confirmed that he was hearing the conversation perfectly well from his seat.

After a couple of hours, I bid him farewell and made promises of coming for a proper visit and to meet his family. As agreed, Alex followed me out of the pub and headed back to the hotel.

We did not discuss Chris until we were at the airport at which point I confessed to being confident that he was genuine. Alex said that he was seventy per cent in agreement; the thirty per cent of doubt was related to how well he seemed to be coping with seeing me after all these years. Alex has spent a lot of time around actors, so he is usually a good judge of character.

At this moment of time, however, the scales are weighing in Chris' favour.

Monday September 12th

Sue is back from holiday and is acting perfectly normally.

I asked how her holiday was and she said it was good, although most of her time was taken catching up on all the chores she has been neglecting for so long. We had a meeting regarding the project and she seems happy with the current progress. It will probably run until the end of the month at which point she will need to present her findings to Darth.

I got home and made some porridge for dinner. I still struggle to make myself proper food when I come in, usually through being too tired. The thought of take away food makes me nauseous. I decided to weigh myself after the porridge to see if it made any difference.

It did not; I am now down to one hundred and thirty two pounds.

Tuesday September 13th

I have always been quite a healthy person and before this year I do not think I had taken a proper sick day for about five years. Today, however, I feel truly awful.

I woke up around four o'clock this morning and immediately threw up in the bathroom. My head is pounding, my throat is in great pain and I feel quite dizzy every time I stand up. I decided that a few days of rest should get me right again, so I set up a make shift bed in the living room.

The few days rest will allow me to watch a number of Hitchcock movies that I have still to see anyway.

Wednesday September 14th

I still feel completely awful.

I can not write more than that.

Thursday September 15th

Now this illness is getting ridiculous.

I do not feel any better than before and now my voice is all but gone.

And I am now going to be sick again.

Friday September 16th

Alex called, but I told him (with some pain) not to come over. He says that his friend is going on a night out with the staff of Evens and Flowers and will call him tomorrow with the information. I asked Alex to come over on Sunday as I will not be getting out of bed until then at least.

I am determined to get rid of this.

Saturday September 17th

Sunday September 18th

I feel a little better today and, although my voice has not returned fully, Alex could at least converse with me (albeit, he did most of the talking). His friend certainly had some interesting information to pass on, although I am not quite sure what to make of it yet.

He has become quite close to Leyton, Mr Flowers and the receptionist Jill. Jill, so we have been informed, is the most interesting of the three to speak to. She has worked at Evens and Flowers for over twenty years, ever since Mr Flowers and Mr Evens went into business together. She has seen all the changes, both good and bad, and has an excellent memory when it comes to her work.

Alex's friend has confided in Jill deliberately, asking her many questions about the culture within the team, the current partners, etc. This, however, was just to build up some confidence before he could approach the subject of Leyton and Sarah. Leyton, according to Jill, is bound to be successful. He works extremely hard and is well liked by both the partners and the staff. Jill believes there may be some history to Leyton, but the firm is only interested in the present.

Alex's friend did not approach the subject of Sarah until the night out and only after Jill had consumed a few glasses of wine. It seems that Sarah was a complete workaholic, loved (rather than liked) by the partners and had her future all lay out in front of her. Jill said the whole practice was shocked when she quit suddenly. The partners believed that she must have been poached by a rival firm, but she just seemed to disappear.

Jill said that she received a Christmas card from her later that same year with a note saying that she was fine and glad to be out of law. There was no address on the note and it was the last she heard of her.

So, unless something comes up next week, it appears that the trail of Sarah has once again gone cold.

Monday September 19th

I feel worse again today, so I have made an appointment with the doctor for tomorrow and now, I am heading back to bed.

Tuesday September 20th

I have both severe throat and chest infections, according to my doctor (who I have not seen for about ten years).

She has given me some antibiotics and signed me off work for a fortnight. She gave me a thorough examination and concluded that my blood pressure is a little high, my weight (one hundred and twenty nine pounds) a little low, and my blood test told her that I needed extra iron. She asked if I was under any stress and I said I was (but chose not to go into any further detail).

I collected my antibiotics and some iron capsules and headed home to call Darth with the good news. To my surprise, she sounded both concerned and caring. She said that she would help out managing the team with Sue and it would be good experience for her.

I called Alex as well and he said that he would come over later on in the week or at the weekend, just as soon as he had heard from his friend in London.

So now, it is off to bed for me once again.

Wednesday September 21st

Thursday September 22nd

Friday September 23rd

I have spent most of the last couple of days in bed.

I am feeling very weak at the moment and it is a real struggle just getting up to eat or go to the toilet. I tried to go for a shower this morning, but I did not have the strength to stand up for longer than a few minutes.

Alex is coming over on Sunday, so I will try and get myself sorted by then.

Saturday September 24th

I had an unexpected visitor today.

My buzzer sounded at around three o'clock this afternoon. I had just gotten dressed, thankfully, having managed a quick shower. The flat was in a mess, as I have had neither the strength nor desire to do anything about it just yet.

I was very surprised to hear anyone call, never mind who is actually was. Without much thought, I let them up and made a pathetic attempt to get the living room in some sort of order in the short time it took them to escalate the stairs.

I had just hidden some dirty underwear under the sofa when the knock on the door came, and I went to open it and let Sue in.

Sunday September 25th

Alex came over with an update from London, but before we get to that I will update you with Sue's visit.

She arrived carrying a box of grapes and a large bottle of Lucazade. She said that she was not sure what to bring for me, however as she thought the last time I was probally sick was back in the nineteen eighties, these items seemed somewhat appropriate (this did make me smile for the first time in days). Sue told me that she had asked Darth for my address and she passed this to Sue with a get well soon message. There was also a signed card from the whole team.

Sue stayed for a couple of hours, filling me in on what I had been missing before insisting on making us both some tea. Luckily I had bought some fresh milk and biscuits on my way back from the doctors or there would have been nothing to offer. I noticed that she started tidying whilst the kettle was boiling, much to my embarrassment. She was sounding very caring when we spoke and I found myself comfortable in her company. I gave her my mobile number when she was leaving and told her that she was welcome back, but to give me some notice next time so I could clean the flat.

When Alex arrived today, he was most interested in the visit. He had also been doing some research of his own and found out something interesting. When I had previously shown him Sue's application, he took some notes of which I took little notice of at the time. On checking some details he found something strange. When Sue came to Edinburgh, she worked for a number of different companies. Of these companies, she spent most time working for one (almost the same length of time as the other companies combined). When Alex then checked her references, there was not one from this particular company. Now it could be coincidence, however, Alex thinks that there may be something there as you would expect to use a reference from a company that you spent most time with. He left this to one side today as he provided an update from London with the information one again coming from Jill.

Jill understands that the partners have agreed to fund Leyton's studies and will be offering him a permanent position upon completion of his degree. Leyton is not currently aware of this; however, Jill firmly believes that he will be ecstatic when he finds out.

Jill also has found out more about Sarah. After the conversation in the pub, she was interested to find out more about what happened to her. She went through some old files that Sarah had been involved in to find details of her cases. From what she could see, Sarah had a one hundred per cent winning record up until her final case before she left the firm. Jill remembers that Sarah had been given a big case (some kind of reputational defence case) that could really have made the name of the practice. As Jill recalls, Sarah lost the case and resigned shortly after. Despite having a good memory, Jill can not recall much about this case as Sarah did not use her much, preferring to do all the work herself.

The strangest thing about the case, however, is that there is no record of it anywhere in the offices of Even and Flowers.

Monday September 26th

Tuesday September 27th

My weight is now one hundred and twenty six pounds and I still do not feel any better.

Wednesday September 28th

Sue called my mobile today to see how I was doing. I said I was a little better today; however, this is not really the case. She asked if she could visit tomorrow as she is finalising the draft of her report to Darth and wanted to discuss it with me first.

Slowly and steadily I spent the rest of the day cleaning the flat, including the dirty underwear still under the sofa.

Thursday September 29th

Sue came over after work and brought dinner with her.

She had picked up some pasta from a local Italian place that I have walked passed many times without venturing in. I am still without an appetite, however, I did manage to eat the whole portion (and I hope that it will not come back to haunt me later).

Sue showed me her report which I read thoroughly. I have done a number of project reports myself and I think that I am rather good at them (certainly when compared to some others I have read), however, Sue's was simply first class. She has obviously spent a lot of time on her research and it read extremely well.

I had little to offer and what changes I did suggest were not major points and more for my ego rather than for drastic improvement. She seemed pleased with my feedback and promised to make the suggested changes.

After a coffee and a chat she left, pausing as she left my flat to kiss me on the cheek.

Friday September 30th

Saturday October 1st

The postman rang my bell at ten o'clock this morning and I did not realise until I opened the door that it would be another parcel.

I called Lars straight away for advice. He confirmed that he was still in his bed in Glasgow. He was due to go out with friends today to attend a Hard Rock Pub Quiz; however, he cancelled this so he could come over to see me and the item. I told him I was feeling quite rough though he was welcome to stay over if he wanted and he said he would bring a change of clothes just in case.

Lars arrived in Edinburgh just after lunchtime and got a taxi straight to my flat. We undertook of the usual greetings and catch up, however, he put his latex gloves on as soon as he had taken off his jacket. Once again I found myself completely frozen to the spot watching his every subtle movement. My current illness is already making my breathing difficult, but at this point it was almost unbearable. I thought at one point I was about to pass out.

Lars examined the parcel thoroughly just as before. It was smaller than the previous one, roughly half the size of a shoe box and cubed in shape. Once again the label looked the same, Lars' only comment during the process was 'same dimples on the label'. He slowly opened the box and pulled out the contents. The item this time looked like a handmade model.

It was a simple framed gallows with a hangman's noose.

Sunday October 2nd

Alex came over today and we spent much of the afternoon pondering over the items that have been sent to me so far.

There are countless meanings for each of the items, on an individual basis, which I commented on at the time I received them. The latest item could also mean a number of things which Alex and I discussed. Obviously, it could relate to hanging, death or punishment. It could also relate to capital punishment (should public hanging be brought back?) or even a crime from a different era. It could also relate to the game hangman where players try to guess a saying or phase by selecting letters before the condemned is drawn. Could it be that the previous items were a clue leading to a game of hangman? Is this the last clue or is there more to come?

Alex and I tried to find anagrams in the previous items but to little success. If you take the words dummy, coffin and scales we found the following words within –

Access, Acid, Unmold, Come, Cliff, Acumen, Amnesic, Amused, Clue, Class, Clumsy, Close, Fly, Made, Maiden, Sadism, Scam, Sly, Suffice.

I am not sure if any of this helps or makes the whole thing even worse. We are also struggling to find a link between the items with the exception of the latest item and the coffin which obviously suggests death.

As you can probably imagine, this is not making me feel any better whatsoever.

Monday October 3rd

I am due to return to work tomorrow and although I do not feel any better I have decided to go anyway.

I called Darth to let her know the good news and she said that she was glad that I was coming back as she had an important discussion to have with Sue and me. It all sounded very intriguing; however, Darth is not one to give anything away.

I guess I will await and see what tomorrow brings.

Tuesday October 4th

As of a half past ten this morning, I am officially unemployed.

I arrived at work early and caught up on my e-mails and messages before speaking to the team about my health, feeling better, ready to get back into the swing of things, etc. It was at ten o'clock this morning that Sue and I headed to Darth's room to find out what was so important. I noticed that Sue was looking a little worried and uncomfortable and I wondered if she knew more than me (although I found out later she did not).

Darth started the meeting by making a long and in depth speech about the changes that were happening in the company, the new vision and strategy that the CEO had delivered and how this was going to impact on our own department. I think this speech went on for about twenty five minutes before the sucker punch came. Going forward there would only be one Senior Underwriter in the department and, as such, Sue and I would have to reapply for our job.

Darth confirmed that she had arranged with the Human Resources department that the appointment would be internal and they would not be considering any other candidates for the role. As she ran through this whole speech, I kept thinking about the threats, the notes, the items sent to me, the attack on me and on Alex. I kept thinking, what is the point of all this if I am going to be killed this year? I stole a glance at Sue and she looked shocked and upset and appeared to have gone very pale in her complexion. I think it was the combination of all these factors which made the words come out of my mouth when I said.

'That will not be necessary Margaret, as I quit'.

Wednesday October 5th

I have never been unemployed before and I do not really know what to expect.

I cleared my desk yesterday and said my goodbyes to the team. I wished Darth all the best for the future and thanked her for all her support over the years. I tried to say goodbye to Sue, but I could tell that she was unsure how to handle the whole situation and I did not want to make her feel any worse.

At this time I cannot even think about another job or what I want to do. I still feel awful, so I will take some time to recover. I weighed myself this morning and found I am still losing weight (now down to one hundred and twenty three pounds) so I do need to try and eat something also. I have thought about taking a trip to Spain to see Dad and Mary, but I will wait until I am feeling better. I spoke to him last night and he seems very happy and settled so I can wait until I feel more up for the trip.

Financially I will fine also. I was well taken care of when mum died (she worked for an insurance company and was obsessed that her family would be well taken care of). I also managed to tackle my drug habit before I smoked my savings away. I own my flat outright and most of my wages, for the last few years, have been transferred to my savings account.

My only concern is with all this free time, I might be making myself much more vulnerable than before.

Thursday October 6th

I got a call from Mike tonight, which is something that I was just not expecting.

I am still upset with everything that happened, but I am just not sure how to react at the moment. Maybe it is my current state of vulnerability, the thought that I could die at any time, but I could not distance myself from him. He has obviously gone through a traumatic time of his own, even if it was self-inflicted, although it could be he was having a breakdown of his own. Mike and I go back a long time and, speaking to him tonight, it seemed like he was more like the Mike I once knew rather than the one who went off the rails this year.

He confirmed that he is heading back up to Edinburgh for a few months. The London office is up and running fully now and performing well above initial expectations. As such, his bosses have requested that he come back to Edinburgh to head up a new project at Head Office. He has also started speaking to Lucy again and, for the sake of Lewis, they are going to try and work things out, He told me he would call again once he was settled.

I decided to call Linda after I hung up the phone as it was imperative that I found out her thoughts. She confessed that Mike had called her on a couple of occasions in the last month or so to apologise and to let her know that he was committed to working things out with his family. Linda does think that it was an affair that got out of hand, on both sides, and for the sake of both Lucy and Lewis she hoped everything worked out for him. She does not think that they will become the best of friends again, but if their paths crossed again she is confident that they would be civil to each other.

I guess that this was the reassurance that I needed should Mike decide to come for a visit.

Friday October 7th

I tried to call D.I. McCreedy today for an update on the case, but as he was unavailable, I spoke to D.S. Stone.

He confirmed that they had a couple of definite lines of enquiry that they were currently following up; however, he could not say any more than that at this time. I was a little comforted by this news which resulted in my confession that I had a few suspects of my own. I suppose that this may have been a little foolish of me but, when questioned further, I told him all about my autobiography and the three suspects. He listened carefully and took the details down. He promised that he would personally look into it further; however, he confirmed that their current lines of enquiry were closer to home.

After the initial comfort of the police finally getting somewhere with the investigation, I am once again feeling more than a little unsettled.

Saturday October 8th

I have not been able to reach Alex today.

I have left a number of messages on his voice mail, but he has not called me back yet.

Sunday October 9th

There is still no news from Alex.

I decided to call Lars, in case he could provide more details regarding my case. He confirmed that he has not spoken to the D.I. or D.S for a few days as he has been focusing on his side of the case. He confirmed that he was still processing the latest item for forensic evidence; however, he has now finished with the scales. He told me that he took apart the packaging and the scales themselves and both were virtually clean. When deconstructing the package, though, he found a small hair which he has sent off for further analysis. He should find out more next week and would let me know.

Are we finally getting somewhere at last, or is this just another dose of false hope?

Monday October 10th

Alex called this morning; he has spent most of the weekend at the police station being questioned about the threats.

When I spoke to him he seemed tired, exhausted even, so I kept the call brief. He said that they wanted to know everything about our friendship, our other friends and associates, how much time we had been spending together recently, etc.

They questioned him from Saturday afternoon through to late evening. They let him home late before bringing him back in on Sunday morning. He was unable to reach his own solicitor, however, the police informed him that they were just gathering information to help with their investigation and he was not a suspect. As such, Alex answered their questions but was surprised at how long they kept him.

When I came off the phone I felt like weeping. I am so scared at the moment and I feel that I am putting Alex at risk as well. With what D.S. Stone told me, I now wonder if they do actually suspect Alex is involved.

I cannot comprehend that he is involved but if he is, I can no longer trust the one person I have complete faith in.

Tuesday October 11th

Sue came over for a visit tonight.

I could tell that she was upset with what had happened and, she told me that she thought it was unfair how things had developed and that she thought that I should have just been given the job. I made some kind of speech about how I wanted to move on anyway, that I was currently looking to explore different avenues within my career and how this could turn out to be a good thing. I am not that sure, though, if I was truly convincing.

I saw that she was close to tears on a number of occasions throughout our discussions and I tried to reassure her by telling her how good she was at her job and how much she had come on, in such a short space of time, since I had first interviewed her. I think I succeeded to some extent as I noticed a smile and an almost bashful look. At this point, it had become more obvious that the discussion had taken a turn. She stared at her lap, fingers twirling her hair in an almost child like manner, as she told me that she would miss working with me. I joked about how it would be no great loss, Sue just shook her head gently and, eyes still fixed on her lap, told me that she had been attracted to me since the first time she had seen me. I laughed this off with some comment about how colleagues should never date and why it never works out in the end, though she just smiled saying that it was maybe a good thing after all that we were no longer colleagues.

She then stood up, walked over to me and we kissed.

Wednesday October 12th

All right, I admit it. I did not see that coming either.

Since I split up with Petra, I have not even thought about another relationship. With everything going on, I just cannot make that kind of commitment at this time. I cannot deny being attracted to Sue, but after the kiss I tried to cool things slightly. I explained about Petra and how I was not ready to start another relationship at the moment. To be fair, Sue was great and completely understanding of my situation. She just asked that we be friends, meet up every once and a while and see how things develop, without any pressure.

I guess that I can live with this, although I am not too sure what Alex will make of it all.

Thursday October 13th

I have not spoken to Alex since he was questioned by the police.

I decided to leave things for just now and wait for him to be ready for the next step. Every time I think that the police may think he is involved, I just cannot seem to be able to get my head round the whole thing. What motive could Alex possibly have? What could I have ever done to upset him? He seems to have helped me at every turn, however, could this really be just a front? Could he really be the world's greatest actor and have orchestrated this whole affair?

Could I have been so stupid to let him?

Friday October 14th

I am meeting with Mike for dinner tonight.

He called to say that he was back living in his Edinburgh flat and wanted to meet up with me alone. He insisted in taking me out as a way of apology, but more so that he could have the opportunity to do so face to face.

I just hope that when I meet him it turns out better than the last time we 'bumped' into each other.

Saturday October 15th

The dinner with Mike went well and I could clearly see the difference in him since the last time we met.

He told me that he could easily blame so many different factors for his previous behaviour. His work - he knew that he was spending too much time there and it was having a serious affect on him. Lucy – she was being overly demanding on his time, wanting him to be at home earlier and for him to spend more time with the family. Lewis – the stress of being a parent with everything else that was happening. Mike even mentioned me – he saw me seemingly strolling through my life without a care in the world.

Mike knew, however, it was all his own doing and no one else could be to blame. He was doing well enough at work and getting the desired results that meant that he could work the hours he chose to. Lucy was right, he should have been spending more time at home and with his family. Lewis is a wonderful child and he did not appreciate how fortunate he was to have a son like him in the first place. He then told me that he took my friendship for granted and, by nearly losing that, he would never forgive himself.

I appreciated the effort and sentiment that Mike had made and I enjoyed the dinner. I even managed to eat a dessert, which was important given the fact I weighed myself before I left. Mike never asked me directly about my weight, but I could tell that he was thinking of it and with good reason.

My weight is now down to one hundred and fifteen pounds.

Sunday October 16th

There is still no word from Alex.

I have spent the whole weekend indoors – I am too scared to venture outside.

I know now, for sure, that anytime I go outside could be my last.

Monday October 17th

Alex and Sue both called me today.

Alex apologised for not calling sooner as he has been working on a new play and he was desperate to get it finished by the end of the weekend. He is very excited about the finished version and already has a number of interested parties. I listened in silence; however, I did not want to hear about his plays right at this moment in time. I was waiting patiently for him to tell me more about the police questioning, but in the end I gave up. I guess he will tell me when he is good and ready, but I am finding the waiting very irritating.

Sue called later this evening to ask how I was feeling (which is completely awful, but I lied again and said I was getting better every day). She told me that the workplace was very strange without me and that the staff members were asking after me. I assume from that last statement that my old colleagues know that Sue is in contact with me.

I am sure that the O.G's love every minute of it.

Tuesday October 18th

Wednesday October 19th

Thursday October 20th

I can not even get out of bed at the moment.

I have made another appointment with the doctor for tomorrow. I have been sick countless times in the last forty eight hours and I have been suffering from chronic diarrhea for weeks now.

Oh, help, here we go again.

Friday October 21st

With great effort I made it out of bed, had a shower and attended my doctor's appointment.

She once again undertook a number of tests and admitted to being slightly alarmed at my weight loss. I am now down to one hundred and eleven pounds which is over a stone in the month since I last saw her. I told her of my lack of appetite and recent susceptibility to regular vomiting. She has prescribed some medicine to assist with the latter. She has also taken some blood for testing and has made a further appointment for two weeks time.

I hope by then she will know exactly what is wrong with me.

Saturday October 22nd

Alex came round today and was visibly upset when he saw me.

'My dear boy, you look thinner than a Hollywood Blockbuster wannabe and whiter than a snow storm in Alaska'.

I told him of my visit to the doctors and that I would know more in a fortnight's time. I was at least glad to report that the medicine was having the desired effect. He was pleased to hear this as he has arranged a party for Halloween and it is 'imperative' that that I be in attendance. He has booked a venue and has some special friends coming, so I cannot let him down.

Alex then proceeded to make some lunch and promised to tell me all about his visit with 'Edinburgh's Finest' if I ate it all (which I just about managed). He confessed to being a little foolish in not having a solicitor present, however, he trusted D.I. McCreedy enough to answer his questions. It seems to Alex that they have a definite suspect and it is not him.

He was surprised at the length of time he was questioned, but they kept confirming that he was not a suspect and his comments would help the case they were building. I asked about the questions themselves and he said they were mainly about my background, my friends and anyone else I am close to. They were not interested in friends or associates from school days and they did not mention the three suspects from my autobiography.

When Alex left, I sat at my table and let everything that Alex said absorb in my head, I am once again convinced that Alex is not involved.

I think that I need to believe this one hundred per cent, if only for the sake of my own sanity.

Sunday October 23rd

I called Alex this morning to tell him straight that he is the only person I trust. I reiterated that if anything should happen to me, he was to take the diary and the contents of my safe and use them to find the perpetrator. I told him it is imperative that he does this for me and I made him promise that he would. He tried to brush this off in his usual manner; however, I could tell from his voice that he was starting to accept that something very well may happen. He made me the promise I needed to hear.

I was surprised to hear my buzzer ringing when I came off the phone. It was Sue and she had arrived with some home made Chicken Soup.

It was good to see her and I was glad for the company. The soup was delicious and she made enough to keep me going for a few days. She told me that she was doing fine at work, although it was more difficult trying to handle double the number of staff. She said that Darth was being very supportive and helping as much as she could until things settle.

I think that with Sue and Darth at the helm, I can see this happening quite quickly.

Monday October 24th

Lars called today with an update to his work to date.

He apologised for not getting back to me sooner, however, he has been working on a double murder case which has just happened (I do recall seeing something on the television recently). He said that there had been no further evidence found, but there was some news on the hair that was found on the third package.

The hair was extensively analysed and was found not to be human, it belonged to a cat.

Tuesday October 25th

D.I. McCreedy called today to ask how I was doing.

I told him that I have been feeling a little under the weather of late and I was awaiting the results of my blood test. He told me that he hoped that everything would turn out well and that he may have some good news for me. He said that they have a definite suspect that they had just brought in for questioning and was hopeful of confirming an arrest soon. I asked if he could confirm who the person in question was and he said that he should not at this time; however, he decided to tell me in strict confidence on the basis that I told no one until the arrest was confirmed.

It is Mike.

Wednesday October 26th

With everything that is happening at this time, I guess I can be excused for not thinking straight.

I called Lars today and asked him to come over. He arrived just after lunch time and joined me for some chicken soup (although he suggested I take the larger portion). Once we had finished, I told him that I was sorry that the only real piece of evidence found was likely to be a dead end. He looked at me strangely and I asked him to follow me. He got up from the table and followed me out the front door to my neighbour's house.

I knocked the door and introduced Lars to Mrs Dunbar and, her cat, Candles.

Thursday October 27th

D.S Stone called me today with a further update.

He confirmed that Mike has now been arrested on the suspicion of the assault (of both me and Alex), threatening behaviour and breach of the peace. He said that they were continuing to question him and had sent their initial report to the Prosecutor Fiscal. Once the confirmation to proceed comes through, they will be setting a date in court.

I am not sure if I could face witnessing such an event, however, I may not have any choice.

Friday October 28th

D.I. McCreedy called to let me know that they have been forced to release Mike on a legal technically.

The Procurator Fiscal did not believe they had a strong enough case to proceed and Mike's solicitor has managed to get him released and all charges dropped. D.I. McCreedy believes that they have found their man, however, would need to continue the investigation. He has warned me not to contact or approach Mike. He asked if I wanted him to arrange police protection, however, I told him that that would not be necessary at this time.

I asked him, more for my own sake, how any of this was possible as it did not make any sense to me whatsoever. He asked me if I was aware of what American's refer to as Means, Motive and Opportunity (which I was, although never paid this much attention to it). He said that Mike certainly had the means - he is intelligent, well connected and wealthy. His motive (the D.I. believes) is simply jealousy – for my relationship with Linda. Finally, Mike had the opportunity – he had access to my flat to post the notes, he was close to me to monitor my movements and the D.I. thinks that he got someone to post the items when he was in London, probably someone from his work's mailroom in Edinburgh. I asked what he thought the meaning of the items was and the D.I. suspects they were red herrings, chosen to unsettle me or suggest suspicion elsewhere.

I was numb when he came off the phone. I just cannot seem to work any of this out.

Saturday October 29th

I have decided to move flat as soon as possible; I cannot stay much longer here.

I have secured a lease on an apartment in St. Andrews and I move in next Friday.

I do not believe I am safe here, although I am also scared to leave.

Mike could get me at anytime.

Sunday October 30th

What if it is not Mike?

What if it is Alex? No, it cannot be Alex, he is my sole allay.

What if it is Sue? Is she really attracted to me? Has she been playing me all along?

What if Leyton is involved after all?

What about Linda? She does not call me often now, could she be involved and I have missed that completely?

I cannot go on like this; I just need to get to Friday. I have not told, or am I going to tell, anyone where I have gone.

I trust no one.

Monday October 31st

Alex's party today – I forgot all about it and he is coming to pick me up at a quarter past ten, which is only twenty five minutes away.

His party is starting at half past ten and he agreed to meet me here before walking to the venue which is quite close. He insisted that I turn up in costume which left me in an awkward position. Fortunately, I have a dinner suit (albeit, it is now far too big for me) so I have decided to go as James Bond. I have a toy pistol and cocktail glass somewhere so I may just get away with it.

I will pop this diary back in the safe now and finish getting ready and see if I can make myself look somewhat presentable for the first time in weeks.

Oh, my buzzer has just gone, I guess Alex is early.

Dearest Uncle,

By the time you read this letter my pain will finally be over. I hope that this note will explain everything to you. All that I can ask, although don't expect to receive, is for your forgiveness for the decision I have made. Words cannot express my gratitude towards you when father died. You were my rock when I needed you and you were also a great support to mother despite the demands of your own family and career.

When I left for London ten years ago, it was not with the aim of finding my dream job as I explained. Although that was to follow, I had an altogether different reason for going. Although I was well taken care of, I have never been able to accept the decision I made all those years ago.

I explained to you, at the time, that my break up with Steve Hamilton was another factor for my leaving Edinburgh and that part was true. I felt that you had carried enough burden since Father died and Mother was never able to recover. My main regret about leaving was my inability to prevent Mother drinking herself into an early grave. She never stopped blaming herself for the accident, despite the many times you tried to explain that she was powerless to prevent the cars crashing.

Although Steve and I were only together for six months (not even enough time for you to meet him), I felt I had found my soul mate. He had also lost a parent and I thought we would be able to help each other. It was his decline into drug use that I could not accept. I thought it was just a phase he was going through, though he never did recover when we were together.

The end came at a night-out together to celebrate our six months anniversary. We ended up in a night club and, I suspected, he had slipped to the toilet to take some drugs. It was not until later I realised how many and the effect that would make on both our lives. The night ended like most couples end their 'special' evenings, however, this was the one time we were unprepared (I shall not go into details). I had had a little too much to drink, so my protestations were weak.

In the cold light of day, we had a blazing row and the relationship ended there and then. I could not accept or understand how selfish he had been the night before and held him fully accountable for his actions. It was not until much later that I admitted to myself that I was just as much to blame as he was. At the time, however, I trusted him enough to love and respect me and he should have been able to accept the fact that I did not want to make love with him that night without the adequate protection.

We did speak a few weeks later and he admitted that he could not remember much of the night in question and apologised profusely, but by then it was too late – I never wanted to see him again. We didn't speak again after that night and I headed to London the next month with a suitcase full of clothes, all my life savings and an unwanted child inside me.

As I said earlier, I was well taken care of at the clinic and the doctors and nurses were so caring. I did spend a number of hours speaking to them about my decision and of the potential regrets I may have in the future, but my mind was made up. I needed to go through with the procedure so I could start to build my life again.

A few weeks after the operation, things started to pick up once more. I applied to three different law firms and was offered a graduate position with them all. I decided to choose the smallest of the three firms as I had the best feeling about them, and I certainly made the correct decision at that time. I was treated like family from the first day and secured a full time role with the practice within eight months.

For the next few years my life was almost perfect. I was thriving in my new job, I had a nice apartment, a couple of good friends and I was settled in London. I dated a few different men over that period, but they didn't work out and I finished the relationships early. Since the termination, I had thought about my decision every day and my regret and repulsiveness towards myself grew stronger as time passed. Then, one day, I was assigned to a case that would change everything forever. I was to represent a client that was suing an abortion clinic, the same clinic that I had used.

To this day, I have told no one of the abortion and I was assigned the case as it had the potential to be ground breaking. The practice's faith in me was astounding and my pride trumped any potential conflict of interest that may have existed. I put everything into that case - blood, sweat, tears and the case took everything out of me. In the end I lost the case and, although the practice never once considered me responsible, I felt wholly to blame. I fully believe I let my emotions get the better of me and I resigned, despite monumental protests from the practice partners, shortly afterwards due to my misgivings.

I had built up a fair amount of savings through a lack of a social life and over working; therefore, I was able to financially support myself as I tried to decide what to do next. This time was the worst of times as I no longer had work to distract me from my emotions and the pain of what I had done grew rapidly after that. The problem is, dear Uncle, I have wanted for nothing but for my pain to end. I tried counselling again, hypnosis, acupuncture even (I was really desperate), but that is it all now, I need to end it myself.

I have read much about suicide and the effects the process has on both the individual and the people around them. It has been known as the 'soft' or 'easy' option but believe me there has been nothing soft or easy about this decision. I have also heard it been referred to as 'a permanent solution to a temporary problem', though there is nothing temporary about my pain. I know other people have been able to deal with their issues; however, I will never be able to do that.

Strangely enough, once I finally made the decision, I now feel totally at ease. I have everything prepared and I will be quite comfortable when it happens. My 'appointment' is booked in for tomorrow, Halloween, which I find somewhat strangely fitting. My final act before tomorrow is writing this letter, as I could not go without letting you know. I have debated for months now about writing this letter and burdening you further with the truth, however, you are the one I person I have been able to trust, the one person who I know will understand. I decided that you should know everything and writing this letter has been a huge comfort in itself.

Thank you so much for everything you have done for me and I hope that you can understand why I have come to this decision. As you know, I was raised with religion; however, at this late stage I truly do not know what awaits me. I just hope for one thing in the afterlife – peace.

You will always be in my heart, dearest Uncle,

Forever grateful,

Sarah x

Monday October 31st – 21:45

Jeff Stone sat in the restaurant, staring at the badly painted ceiling, thinking. Timing, it all came down to timing. The time he had spent planning everything to the last possible detail was now approaching twelve months. Twelve months, much sooner than most people would have been able to manage. Then again, he has forty years experience to help him cover his tracks.

'Are you alright, dear?' his wife asked from across the table.

He smiled and nodded, touching her hand gently in confirmation. Yes, he was alright and in half an hour he would finally be content. He had spent forty years playing the bad guy, the tough police officer, but out of hours he was completely different. Yes, family meant everything to Jeff which is why he was going ahead with what he was now preparing to do.

Jeff looked over at his wife again.

'Darling, I have just remembered. I have bought you a present but I have left it in the car. Could you order the cheesecake for me and I will nip to the car to get it? I will only be ten minutes.'

'Of course, dear', she replied smiling.

A quick glance at the restaurant clock told him it was 21:50. The time was perfect, second precision even.

Jeff turned the corner from the restaurant and ran to the car which was parked outside the flat in question. Everything planned. Jeff was nearly sixty years old, retirement was upon him in the coming weeks, but he kept himself in great shape. He was hardly out of breath when he opened the boot of the car and took out his rucksack. Wearing gloves to keep out the cold and evidence, he pressed the buzzer to Steve's flat. He was let inside without question and Jeff quickly put on his forensic suit he had taken from the rucksack once safely inside the stair well and out of view of passers by. He pulled over his hood, lifted the mask over his face and held the baseball bat loosely in his powerful hand. He knew Steve had not got round to getting a spy hole installed in his front door, so the door would be open without question.

Jeff knocked gently on the door and awaited the reply. Everything from there was perfect.

Steve opened the door without looking and turned to walk back inside. One shot was all Jeff could afford – he could not afford a lot of blood. He knew exactly where to strike and Steve fell instantly onto the soft carpet of his living room. Jeff bent down to check for a pulse and was able to confirm that he had been successful. He quickly retreated from the flat, carefully placing the suit and weapon in his rucksack. No one was around as he placed these back into his boot and picked up his wife's present. Time check – 21:57, perfect.

He ran back towards the restaurant, stopping at the corner and taking a few deep breaths before walking back to the table with gift in hand. Restaurant clock 21:59, to perfection. Jeff had to focus hard on his wife as she opened the present, finishing the last of her wine. He took a large drink from his still mineral water and started to relax.

His mind started to wander again, thinking of the last twelve months and the planning he had made. He wanted to make Steve suffer, that was key to the whole affair. Jeff could have had him killed but the knowing that he was going to be killed, that would have made it much worse for him. Since receiving the letter from Sarah, he was able to track down Steve quickly (careful to cover his tracks) and had completed his research before Christmas last year. The notes started it all off, kept initially a month apart to ease it in gently. He did not want to send too many, he did not want to make any mistakes especially before he had really started.

The attacks were a risk, but a necessary and calculated risk. He needed it to be reported to the police so that he could keep a closer eye on what was happening. He knew that it would come to D.I. McCreedy and himself anyway, the fact that Steve knew the Danish forensic guy was just chance. He had planned on implementing one of his friends, Mike being the perfect suspect due to their falling out. If he had more time he could have built a stronger case, he was not surprised that the Procurator Fiscal threw it out. That was not a real issue; he just had to keep things moving slowly until tonight and his pending retirement.

The items were fun, but also necessity. He did this for his own benefit but also to make out it was some sort of mad man, rather than a sane police officer with forty years service and an exemplary record. The items were chosen with care, both for meaning and forensically. All were sourced carefully with the items all mass produced and bought from a shop with no

CCTV. They were paid for in cash by a homeless junkie he had in turn paid to buy the items for him.

The dummy represented Steve unborn child that his beloved Sarah was forced to terminate. The coffin represented Sarah's death which was as a direct result of the termination. The scales represented justice and his determination that it be served. Finally, the gallows represented the punishment which he had just served.

His only concern came when Steve called with his three suspects which included Sarah. It was fortunate that he had answered the phone and taken the details of the three. This meant that he had to proceed with tonight a little earlier than expected; however, he had every last detail planned so moving it forward by a few weeks was not a problem. The information he gained on the telephone that day was not shared with anyone else.

Jeff was just finishing off the cheesecake, despite his lack of appetite, when his phone rang. He passed an apologetic look to his wife as he stepped outside to speak to D.I. McCreedy once again noting the restaurant clock – 22:19.

'I'm sorry love, something terrible has happened. Will you be alright getting a taxi back?' he asked upon his return.

His wife, as always, was completely compliant. She had over thirty year's policeman's wife experience and was looking forward to getting her husband back after all these years. 'Retirement is just around the corner' he kept saying to her this year and she knew it was not long now. He had hinted at buying a villa in Portugal when his pension came through, which would be a perfect escape for them both. He never discussed his cases at home and she never asked.

Jeff knew that this would likely be his final crime scene and any traces left would be put down to his appearance at the crime scene. He would be first to arrive, all planned to perfection, and he would be able to cover his tracks.

And the murder weapon would remain in his boot with his suit and mask, where no one would look, until he could destroy the evidence at a later time.

Everything planned to perfection…

Monday October 31st – 22:15

Alex arrived as planned just before a quarter past ten for the party. He brought the set of keys that Steve had given him to let himself in (he normally rang the buzzer, but he wanted to surprise Steve with his costume). Alex was determined to use tonight as the opportunity to forget everything that had happened and just enjoy themselves. Despite the obvious breakdown Steve had experienced, Alex knew that he was the one person who could help keep him together. Alex felt they were getting close to a resolution ('they' meaning the police) and it would not be long.

Alex ascended the last of the stairs and pushed the key into the lock. He wondered if Steve had decided to dress up as instructed or whether he would not bother. He gave the door a gentle push and, preparing to announce his arrival, he froze in his tracks. It was maybe only a few seconds, however, it felt like it took a lifetime for the scene in front of him to register. He knew his friend was dead long before he reached down and established that he had no pulse. Alex immediately stepped over to the safe; he had to compose himself for the sake of his friend and fulfil his promise.

Steve had been very clear with his instructions, open the safe and remove everything inside. Alex quickly opened it, using the key he had been given, and found a stamped envelope addressed to his home address. The envelope contained the diary, a notebook, a copy of the autobiography, a large sum of cash (which Alex was not expecting) and what appeared to be a note from Steve. Again following his friends instruction, he sealed the envelope and headed back to the main door. The post box was just outside; Alex dropped the package inside and, following a deep breath, telephoned D.I. McCreedy.

'It is regarding Steve, I think you have been too late'.

LOTHIAN & BORDERS POLICE
CRIME REPORT
REF – PJ20/10 – 03/02/2012

AUTHOR – D.I EDWARD MCCREEDY

Death of Stephen James Hamilton – 31/10/2011

The body of the deceased was found at approximately 22:15 on the day of the thirty first of October in the year of two thousand and eleven by Alexander Simpson, an associate of the deceased. An emergency call was placed thereafter, directly to me, by Mr Simpson as I was senior officer in charge of an ongoing investigation into threats made on the deceased. As Mr Simpson was believed to be an assault victim related to these threats, he was already in possession of my contact information.

The first officer on the scene was Detective Sergeant Jeffery Stone (now retired) who was dining in a nearby restaurant at the time of the call. As D.S. Stone was also involved in the investigation, he attended the scene shortly before I arrived. D.S. Stone was able to confirm that Mr Hamilton was deceased and arranged a local doctor to be called to confirm life extinct. D.S. Stone also arranged for the pathologist, Dr Jane Grant, and SOCO's to be in attendance.

D.S. Stone awaited my arrival before we interviewed Mr Simpson who was visibly in shock and distressed by the events. Mr Simpson had made arrangements to meet with the deceased that evening. Mr Simpson is in possession of keys to the apartment and was able to let himself in, when there was no reply to his knocking, thereafter finding the body of the deceased. Upon seeing the deceased, and confirming there was no sign of a pulse, Mr Simpson ran from the apartment before calling me. Mr Simpson was only able to return to the apartment once D.S. Stone was in attendance.

The SOCO's confirmed that there was no sign of forced entry, and no obvious forensic evidence has been discovered as yet. The apartment was searched and there was no sign of anything missing, however, a safe belonging to the deceased was discovered in the bedroom cupboard. A Police appointed locksmith forced the safe open and it was found to be empty.

Dr Grant has since confirmed that death was as a result of a single blow to the back of the skull with a large rounded object. Despite an extensive search of the apartment, and surrounding area, the murder weapon has still to be located.

At this time the case remains open as the investigation into the murder of Stephen James Hamilton, by person or persons unknown, continues.

Printed in Great Britain
by Amazon